S0-CAB-977

"I'm so...ready," Tina breathed

Tyler sucked in a breath at the sight of those heavy eyes and slick mouth. He had to clench his hands to keep from reaching out and touching her.

"Lead the way." Tyler just hoped Tina didn't notice that his voice sounded different from the stripper's. At least the mask covering his face would help hide his identity. If she found out who he *really* was, she'd kill him.

"My pleasure." She took his arm and led him to the hotel elevators.

He should have felt stupid dressed in a leather costume impersonating a stripper, but Tina's reaction had him getting into the part, especially when the elevator doors closed and she boldly reached around to squeeze his buns.

"You must work out." She pressed her hips against his. "I thought we might have a little workout session of our own."

"I don't mind getting a little physical after a performance, especially with such an exceptionally beautiful woman."

And that's exactly what Tyler wanted—to get her into bed, any way he could. And it looked as if he was about to succeed beyond his wildest dreams....

Blaze™

Dear Reader,

Tina Henderson isn't considered The Shark for nothing! And it's not just her cutthroat career as a hotshot lawyer that earned her the title. Because Tina has a way of getting her teeth into a guy, mauling him and then leaving him to bleed out in the water.

But Tyler is a different kind of man, the kind any woman would want to sink her teeth into...then savor. After all, the man can impersonate a stripper as if he was born to the role, and his lovemaking technique is definitely unique, often involving lobster and lots of butter.

Tina still has a few life lessons to learn. She's got to let loose of her famous self-control, her expensive shoes and all of her attitude, and let Tyler nibble his way under her shell.

It just goes to show that a modern girl can be tough, but tender with the right condiments.

Enjoy,

Mara Fox

LETTING LOOSE!
Mara Fox

HARLEQUIN®

TORONTO • NEW YORK • LONDON
AMSTERDAM • PARIS • SYDNEY • HAMBURG
STOCKHOLM • ATHENS • TOKYO • MILAN • MADRID
PRAGUE • WARSAW • BUDAPEST • AUCKLAND

If you purchased this book without a cover you should be aware
that this book is stolen property. It was reported as "unsold and
destroyed" to the publisher, and neither the author nor the
publisher has received any payment for this "stripped book."

ISBN-13: 978-0-373-79302-0
ISBN-10:   0-373-79302-2

LETTING LOOSE!

Copyright © 2007 by Mara Fox Horstman.

All rights reserved. Except for use in any review, the reproduction or
utilization of this work in whole or in part in any form by any electronic,
mechanical or other means, now known or hereafter invented, including
xerography, photocopying and recording, or in any information storage
or retrieval system, is forbidden without the written permission of the
publisher, Harlequin Enterprises Limited, 225 Duncan Mill Road,
Don Mills, Ontario, Canada M3B 3K9.

All characters in this book have no existence outside the imagination of the
author and have no relation whatsoever to anyone bearing the same
name or names. They are not even distantly inspired by any individual
known or unknown to the author, and all incidents are pure invention.

This edition published by arrangement with Harlequin Books S.A.

® and TM are trademarks of the publisher. Trademarks indicated with
® are registered in the United States Patent and Trademark Office, the
Canadian Trade Marks Office and in other countries.

www.eHarlequin.com

Printed in U.S.A.

ABOUT THE AUTHOR

As a former military brat who spent a lot of time in California and also a military wife stationed in the beautiful state of Hawaii, Mara has a special love for the coast and beaches, where she set both of her Harlequin Blaze novels, *Letting Go!* and *Letting Loose!* Especially since she ended up settling far away from those beaches in Texas hill country... However, she claims there are compensations; she's got a boyfriend who is a real cowboy and an inspiration. She loves to swim, read and ride. She enjoys sunsets more than sunrises because she likes to sleep in. Presently, in addition to going back to college, she's raising children, calves and golden retriever puppies.

Books by Mara Fox
HARLEQUIN BLAZE
257—LETTING GO!

HARLEQUIN TEMPTATION
982—I SHOCKED THE SHERIFF

Don't miss any of our special offers. Write to us at the following address for information on our newest releases.

Harlequin Reader Service
U.S.: 3010 Walden Ave., P.O. Box 1325, Buffalo, NY 14269
Canadian: P.O. Box 609, Fort Erie, Ont. L2A 5X3

I dedicate this book to Kate Schaefer, the strongest woman in my life—a mom who held it all together for her three kids, went to school at night, worked all day and still had time to make us feel as if we were the most important people in her world. She could do anything and she proved it whenever our lives got tough. When Lil Kate had cancer she never missed a surgery or a long day of chemotherapy— she fought for Lil Kate's life by my side.

Mama—I can never give you what you've given me. But I can tell you how much you mean to me and how you inspire my writing.

I love you so much. This one's for you.

Prologue

"WHAT DO YOU MEAN you aren't going to have a traditional bachelorette party?" Tina Henderson wiped the perspiration from her neck and nearly bare breasts with a swipe from her towel. "I've got the most magnificent stripper in mind for the party. He's called 'The Bandit.'" She leaned forward and added in a stage whisper, "And he's hung like a stallion."

"I'm not going anywhere near some naked male stranger when I'm about to be married," Emma Daniels protested vigorously.

"Okay, okay, fine, Emma—though it's too bad since you're going to be stuck with the same sex partner for the rest of your life." Tina shuddered.

"Just think how good we'll get at pleasing each other sexually," Emma said with a confidence she hadn't had months ago, before her cruise of self-discovery. During a little jaunt to the Bahamas, she'd discovered her sensual self with the help of a handsome boy toy. A man who had turned out to be not just a toy, but Mr. Right.

Except, Tina didn't really believe there was a right

guy…only the right guy for the moment. Mr. Right Now. "You were coming out of your shell so well, having fun, meeting people. When you fell in love you reverted back to your uptight self," she complained.

"No, I committed. And it's amazing."

But Emma's bold talk was spoiled when a man entered the coed sauna and she immediately adjusted her towel to cover her thong.

Sometimes, Emma still acted like the girl next door.

"This stripper's amazing," Tina coaxed. "You'll regret it if you don't have him at your party—" she winked "—or just *have* him."

"Even you wouldn't do that."

Tina mopped some sweat off her arm. "Be careful. You know that I'll do just about anything." Her attention wandered when a man stripped down to a thong and displayed a rather stunning set of abs.

"Hello? Tina, are you paying attention? No stripper. In fact, I'm having a coed bachelorette party."

"It's rather inconvenient, you acquiring a backbone now, when I've got my heart set on The Bandit."

"Your heart isn't set on anything, only your libido."

"That hurts." She shrugged. "But it's true. Take that man who just came into the sauna."

"The one you've been drooling over?"

"Absolutely. My libido is definitely set on that guy." Tina smiled, and then slowly uncrossed her legs and casually adjusted her thong.

"You may have to cut short your own little strip-tease. It appears his girlfriend has come to save him."

"Damn." Tina shrugged as the woman settled herself beside the man with a proprietary air.

"You are so naughty. What have you got against relationships, anyway?"

"Have you seen the divorce statistics? Divorce is what keeps us lawyers in four-hundred-dollar shoes." She wriggled her manicured toes.

"Stop being so cynical. If half of all marriages fail, that means half of them last forever," Emma insisted. "Look at how understanding Tony was about my fertility problem. We're going to last forever, for sure."

"I guess that's the glass-is-half-full way to look at the divorce statistics. And Tony was pretty good about that. Of course, if he hadn't been, I was prepared to do something drastic," Tina teased. She actually liked it when Emma stood up to her. "But it's safer and a whole lot cheaper if you just play the field." Tina preened for the man whose gaze kept straying to her toned body, despite that he was spoken for.

"I know you're cynical because of your job," Emma said, waving off Tina's immediate protest, "and because of being bounced around during your childhood. But you had enough faith to put yourself through school, and then make something of your life. Why is it so hard to believe in love?"

"I could love an unlimited supply of designer shoes, I think, although my attention span is woefully short."

Emma just smiled that annoying I'm-your-best-friend-who-knows-you-better-than-you-know-yourself smile.

Tina wondered how a loner like herself had ever ended up with a best friend. Emma had sort of snuck up on her.

"How is Tyler? What kinda cases is he taking these days?" Emma said with another one of those stupid smiles.

"Criminal cases, I imagine, since that's what he does." Tina gave the ab man a teasing smile, and then shrugged so her erect nipples pressed against the thin material of her top. She didn't have many inhibitions: where she'd grown up there had been no privacy, no room to herself, no real parents to look after her. She'd had to fight for anything she'd wanted, using her brain, and later her body, to her advantage.

"Stop that."

"Stop what?"

Emma straightened up. "Stop flirting with someone else's boyfriend. She's going to attack you with those lethal-looking fingernails."

"I'll bet my manicure against her manicure any day."

"You won't be as pretty with bloody gouges on your face. Besides, there might be a weapon under that towel."

"The only thing she's hiding under there is cellulite. What does she expect? She should go work out. Why should I sweat at the gym, and then hide my body just to make her feel good?" Tina's voice got a little shrill. Lately, she'd been going to the gym just to kill time, and to try to get rid of the lethargy dogging her evenings.

Emma held up a hand. "Shhh. What's wrong with

you? Since when do you have to poach? You usually only act like that when you're pissed off, and since talking about Tyler seems to piss you off, I think you might consider the ramifications, counselor."

"Ramifications?" Tina rubbed her index finger and her middle finger together, a nervous habit she hated. She never thought about Tyler. He'd overstepped her careful boundaries, for which he'd been banished, and then buried, as deeply as all the rest of the shit in her past.

"Okay, ignore the obvious if you think you can. You may not care about romance, but I want it, all of it. And I don't want to ruin this special time by spending the evening of my party watching some stripper and throwing up on my best friend."

"Well, thanks for thinking of me, but I'd rather get stinking drunk than get caught up in any romance." Tina shuddered for effect, making her breasts giggle. The man across the sauna made eye contact with her chest, making her grin. His girlfriend grabbed his arm, muttered something in his ear and then pulled him to his feet.

"That wasn't nice."

"I'm in a rut, and he looked like he could pull me out. It's frustrating—my job's going great, and I'm still restless. What's wrong with me?"

"Nothing a relationship with Mr. Right wouldn't cure."

"Right. I'll take The Bandit."

"That's not a relationship. You're dangerous in this mood. That poor guy is going to get it from his girlfriend. She couldn't wait to get him outta here."

"I can't help it."

"Just try to concentrate on the party, okay? This is my night, so I get what I want. And I want a cruise theme." She blew out a breath. "Tony's family is huge, and we're going to be inundated with them." She eyed Tina. "But the more the merrier, so if you want to invite…"

She knew whom Emma would suggest she invite if Tina allowed her to continue. "We can start on the beach, and then move the later portion of the party to a nice inside suite. The guests who are interested can get rooms for the evening. And your hair won't get all frizzy."

Emma ran a hand tentatively through her hair.

Tina smiled. Mentioning frizz usually distracted Emma from those topics Tina most wanted to avoid.

"A bonfire with those flaming torches would be nice," Emma said, sounding wistful. "It would be informal and fun."

Tina resisted the urge to sigh.

"We could go for a walk in the moonlight."

When Emma got that distant look, Tina knew she was remembering the beach where she'd met Tony. It wasn't hard to see the magic between them.

I'm not jealous. "Everyone will be waiting for the falling-down-drunk part of the party, so we should at least get them started with those drinks mixed in coconuts."

Emma shook her head. "Not everyone will be looking to get drunk."

"Yeah, well, without The Bandit, you need to spice

up the party somehow. You'll regret not having him. Believe me, it would make it a memorable evening. One fortunate lady might have even gotten lucky with him."

"No one sleeps with a stripper—especially not you. You're not desperate. You're just in a little rut."

"Thanks." Ever since the cruise, when Emma's life had fallen into place, Tina's seemed to have fallen apart. She couldn't seem to find a man to satisfy her.

"Maybe you'll meet someone at the party." Emma patted her arm, and Tina resisted the urge to pull away. She wasn't used to sympathy, and usually resented it. But for some reason, Emma mattered to her.

And it still surprised the hell out of her.

"What? And have the night ruined? There are rules against men interfering with our female fun, you know."

"Since when are you a stickler for rules? I agree that the girls should have a little fun, but no strippers. Promise me."

Tina rubbed her fingers together. It was an old nervous habit she'd thought she'd conquered. It certainly wasn't appropriate for a hotshot lawyer who looked to make partner in Jacksonville's biggest law firm. She glanced down at her fancy manicure and realized that technically, her fingers were crossed.

"Tina, promise me!"

Those naughty fingers, Tina grinned.

"Okay, I promise."

1

"TINA, THAT STRIPPER'S amazing. What an ass. And those abs. It's amazing what little strips of leather can do for a man. I just wish I had the chance to tear off all that leather—with my teeth." Lindsay bared her perfect pearly whites.

Tina noted that Lindsay's toothy smile looked almost feral in her pinched, anorexic face.

"Here's to men in leather." Lindsay raised her glass in a mock toast, expensive rings sparkling on every one of her bony fingers.

The Bandit certainly had Tina's vote, and between his gyrations and the leather straps shifting over his tan muscles, he certainly had everyone's attention.

Tina blurrily considered that she was almost drunk.

Good thing, too, because Emma's usually placid eyes were the color of a storm at sea. Tony could be seen trying to calm her, but Tina knew she was in trouble for hiring The Bandit, and then sneaking him into the hotel with all those luscious leather straps hidden under a trench coat.

Lindsay was right. Leather made a man hot.

Tina was also hot.

She'd been fired up all the way into the hotel after the dinner and the bonfire. But only because The Bandit was due to arrive.

Maybe she should have taken The Bandit directly to her hotel room: gotten sweaty and mussed while taking off each section of leather, piece by piece, inch by sexy inch—instead of hanging here with all of these *couples*.

She didn't do the couple thing. After they'd had a wonderful time on the cruise, Tyler seemed to have that couple's thing in mind, and she'd nixed it…after letting him get embarrassingly close.

He'd been the first man to actually spend the whole night at her place. And she didn't do that sort of thing. No matter how good the sex, the guy went home after. She might stay over at his place, but rarely. She didn't like the morning-after awkwardness or the intimacy.

Unwillingly, her eyes strayed to the corner where Tyler sat with an attractive woman perched practically on his lap; obstinately, she refused to look away when those blue eyes challenged.

She never backed down from a challenge.

And getting a professional stripper into her bed was going to be something. The Bandit would definitely make her forget anything she might feel for Tyler.

Tina looked over at Emma and Tony again. Didn't they know what a mistake they were making? From what she'd seen growing up, there was no such thing as a couple. Just two people unwilling to admit they would eventually get tired of each other, get tired of having sex with each other.

Emma finally broke away from Tony, and then got directly in Tina's face.

"Why did you bring him?" Emma gestured with her chin. "You promised," she hissed.

In a sexy little bronze dress with a plunging neckline embroidered in gold, Emma looked great.

Too bad it wasn't The Bandit kind of hot.

But the neckline of her flimsy dress was suspiciously askew and Emma's nipples were at attention. Tina suspected Tony had very recently had his clever fingers deep inside the silk. "Aren't you glad you didn't wear the bra?"

Emma blushed. "Yes, he definitely likes the dress."

"What's not to like? But it's the boobs, not the dress he's enamored with."

One of the girls gathered around The Bandit actually moaned.

Emma resumed looking disgusted. "How could you do this?"

"I had my fingers crossed when I promised. You know I do that sometimes."

"So it's my fault because I didn't look at your damn fingers? Is this part of the I-don't-understand-how-friendship-works problem? Or is it about your recent troubles with your social life?" Emma looked really upset and worried.

Tina's gut rolled, and she didn't know if it was from the alcohol or the hurt look on Emma's face. Emma was a good friend, one of the few people Tina trusted, and she'd gone and blown it because…well, for no good reason. "I'm sorry. I'll take him away in a few minutes."

"What are we going to tell the girls? And how much did you pay? I mean, I don't want you to be out a lot of money…" Emma's eyes widened as she saw him caressing the leather shield in front of his groin. "He can't be built like that? It's padding, or something. Right?" Her voice rose.

"Watch out, honey. You're drooling, and Tony's watching. Don't worry about the money or that equipment going to waste. I have every intention of taking him to my room and stripping him down to the bare essentials. I'll give you a blow by blow in the morning, so to speak."

"Tina, you can't have sex with a stripper. What are you thinking?"

"Of course I can." She looked toward the corner.

Emma noticed right away. "I'm sorry. I had no idea Sheila would hook Tyler for the evening."

There was another half scream, half sob from the women watching the stripper. Tina saw one of the paralegals from work stuff a bill in his thong. "Why would I pine for a regular man when I can have a little party of my own with The Bandit? I've been thinking about this guy since he came to my friend's party last month. Now I'm gonna put all of my curiosity to bed, and let that fantasy throw me over its shoulder and carry me away."

Emma shook her head. "I don't think it's a good

idea. But I have to admit, I'm glad he's not going to be staying for the whole party. I think Tony's going to have a fit. He wouldn't have minded if I had a stripper. He's just not comfortable watching, and neither am I."

"Just think how desperate he'll be to please you after seeing the competition. He's gonna put both hands down into that dress."

Emma blushed. "I'm still not pleased that you broke your promise. But I'm not going to tell Tony anything except that the girls at the office insisted we invite a stripper as a joke, so long as you get him out of here so it's not obvious that you brought him along for the evening. You know The Bandit may not sleep with you. He's a stripper, not a prostitute."

"I'll be very persuasive. I'm sure I'm not the first client who wanted a little something extra."

Emma shivered. "Be careful. You don't know what you're getting yourself into." She shook her head as if to clear it. "I'd better get back to Tony."

Tina started breathing again. Miraculously, Emma was going to forgive her, again. "You do that. I'm gonna get another drink and let the girls have just a few more minutes of The Bandit's time before I whisk him away to be my own little plaything." Tina headed for the bar where one of her favorite judges was waiting in line. They did a little verbal sparring—it wouldn't have been sporting otherwise. And then Tina wandered to the outskirts of the group worshipping The Bandit.

Let them grope him.

She could afford to be generous when she was the one who would be with him at the end of the night.

The girls were giving him a good time, but the stripper gave her a wink as she settled on a chair. She knew it was part of the act but she was prepared to offer him quite a sum. And while she'd never paid for sex before, she didn't think a stripper would protest too much.

TYLER WALDEN finally escaped Sheila's wandering hands, and then made his way to the balcony where he could look out over the tree line. He took a deep breath. It was difficult watching Tina drooling over the stripper. He wiped his brow. Funny how he could maintain icy control in the courtroom, but have Tina waltz into any other room and he couldn't think straight.

"Tough, huh?" His best friend, Nelson, joined him after carefully shutting the French doors behind them. Perspiration dotted the bald spot on Nelson's head and his fine blond hair. "It's hot in there."

"In more ways than one." Tyler smiled halfheartedly.

Nelson took off his glasses and wiped them on his shirt. "If only she'd look at you like she looks at him. Instead, she's staring a hole right through you."

"No chance of her looking at me that way."

"That's because you're not prancing around in leather. But I bet you're just as fit as that guy—now that you spend all your time at the gym instead of out having a beer with me." Nelson patted his overflowing middle.

Tyler smiled at his buddy, but the grin quickly

faded. "I think she's actually contemplating sleeping with that stripper."

"Naw, women only look at strippers. They don't touch." Nelson made a motion like that of the gyrating stripper.

"She has a very determined look in her eye. I know that look."

Tyler had never felt jealous in his life, especially jealous of some low-life stripper. But the green monster was alive and kicking inside him now. "Apparently, it's really over between us. She isn't interested in me. She's interested in…" Tyler gestured toward the room where they could still see the women and the stripper through the glass. "Maybe I need a change of scenery. I could go home to Georgia. Then I wouldn't have to see her so often."

"Wait a minute, pal. Before you contemplate a change of state, I think you should know that she's going to be disappointed if she finally gets into his pants. The guy's obviously heavily padded. She's going to be paying a fortune to spend her evening with a cotton lining."

"Why should I care?" Tyler turned his back on the doors.

"You could have her tonight." His friend's blue eyes were earnest behind his glasses.

"I'd have to knock her out and carry her out of the room. The only way she'd let me touch her again is if she were unconscious."

"Naw. That would only aggravate your old football

injury. Let's face it, guy, you've got a bad back. I've got a better idea." Nelson's face suddenly turned mischievous. He punched his friend in the shoulder and said, "You should switch with the stripper. Then you can hook into this fantasy. If it's good enough, she might take you back. And if not—" he shrugged "—then you nailed her one last time."

"Nelson, you've got to be kidding me. That's damn desperate, not to mention disgusting."

"Yeah, and what are you if not damn desperate? You've been crying over her for months now, ever since just after the cruise."

"I am not crying."

"You do everything but. What about the woman has you so tied up in knots?"

"She wanted me on the cruise. We had a great time. Conversation, chemistry, sex, we had it all. Then we come back, we have a few great dates, and then *bam,* she literally slams her door in my face. No reason. It's just over. She doesn't do relationships. No foul, it's just over." He shook his head. "But it's not over for me."

Nelson just looked pointedly at the stripper.

"I'm not that desperate."

"Okay." Nelson turned to go. "It's your funeral."

Tyler shook his head. "What makes you think I could impersonate a stripper?"

"Got a cock?"

Tyler sighed. "I mean, how am I supposed to arrange to trade places with him? And then how am I supposed to convince Tina that I'm The Bandit? We've been together before."

"Just as long as the alcohol keeps flowing, she won't be as sharp as usual. As for the costume, just offer bandit boy a couple of hundred dollars for the leather straps and mask. He'll probably jump at the opportunity to make a fast buck. If you're wearing that mask, she'll never see who she's really with. This is the moment when all the extra time you've put in at the gym trying to forget her pays off."

Tyler grabbed the iron railing in a hard grip. While he usually trusted Nelson's judgment, this was outrageous. "This is nuts." Tyler ran his fingers through his hair. "It's playing with her life, real life, and she'll probably hate me in the morning."

Assuming I can pull off being a stripper.

Nelson fiddled with his watch. "I don't think it's a huge risk. Tina likes a little spice in her life. She might be intrigued enough to give you another shot, or she might be aroused enough to keep you busy for the rest of the weekend. Or…"

"Or?"

"Or she might give you a black eye."

"She might do more than give me a black eye. She's certainly the toughest woman I've ever met." Tyler rubbed his face as if he could already feel the bruises.

"Yeah, can't figure why you've got it so badly for her, other than the body, I mean. She's earned her reputation."

"You mean *The Shark* thing? She's an enigma, that's for sure—a woman who looks like a debutante and swears like a soldier," Tyler mused. "I remember when she actually stared down a client's abusive husband who confronted her with a gun outside of the courtroom. Next day, she waltzed with the governor at a fund-raiser, and got her picture in the paper. She's amazing."

"So she's tough, and she cleans up nicely. My assistant claims she spends a fortune to get her hair done. She's catty."

"Which one?" Tyler asked.

Nelson chortled. "Both of them. Beth's overfed and grumpy. And Tina, she's like a sleek little Egyptian cat. But her claws are lethal."

Tyler shrugged. "What's interesting about being sweet and nice?"

"She's as hard as they come. No softer emotions. I just don't find that especially attractive in a woman."

Tyler barely paid attention to Nelson's observations. Everyone said the same thing: Tina was a fantastic lawyer, and a hell of a lay, for those lucky enough to have been singled out, but not sympathetic, and certainly not relationship material. But people were his specialty, and he saw something in her that she tried hard to hide. Call it vulnerability. Call it bravado. The woman had serious depth.

"There's more to her than meets the eye. Some of her clients are real charity cases, which means she isn't representing everyone just for the money. There's another motivation. One I don't understand yet."

"So she takes on pro bono. Everyone decent does. But you never see her clients turn to her and give her a hug."

"No, she definitely doesn't invite hugs." Tyler grinned. He didn't know why he found it amusing, the way Tina intimidated everyone. He had a feeling she worked at it. "She's fascinating, full of contradictions. She's the most amazing puzzle. Where does she come from? And why is she so scary?"

"Hey, I'm not knocking her. She's a fantastic lawyer." Nelson ran his hand over his thinning hair. "And I have an ulterior motive. I'm confident that when you get to see her as much as you want, you'll eventually get tired of her. Just like all the other women you've dated. Then maybe you'll stop moping. I was the one who encouraged you to go on that cruise, so I feel obligated to help you out now."

"I do not mope."

"Could have fooled me."

"I'm just confused. I've never been tied in knots by a woman, didn't even know what it meant."

"You don't have to stay confused. Do some research, run a background check. That ought to solve the mystery that is Tina Henderson so you can get on with your life. And I can get on with mine." Nelson tipped his head toward the doors.

"That wouldn't be sporting. The kind of research I want to do is up close and personal. I want her to tell me everything with her hair spread out on my pillow."

"That sounds like the old you—I guess there's hope for you yet. Maybe you should follow her around. Find out what she's doing. James Bond stuff."

Tyler turned and his eyes met Tina's cool, assessing gaze as if there weren't a room, a crowd, and a piece of glass between them. Then she dismissed him to look back at the stripper.

He knew he would never get to Tina by normal means: flowers, candy or romance, the things that all the other women in his life had wanted.

Not Tina. He'd tried everything from roses to orchids. He'd sent tickets for opera performances and basketball games. She'd even sent back the little lawyer bear he'd had made especially for her. For once in his life, something hadn't fallen into place. She hadn't gone out with him since the night she'd let him stay over at her place.

He couldn't stop thinking about her. She was the one challenge he hadn't mastered. She'd barely given him a chance. So what did he have to lose? Just his reputation and his pride. "It's a crazy idea, me impersonating a stripper. Can you imagine what would happen if anyone ever found out?"

"You can't be disbarred for fulfilling a sexual fantasy in the privacy of a hotel room."

"She'll laugh at me."

"I don't think she has your sense of humor. Either she'll be intrigued, or angry." Nelson put his hand on Tyler's arm. "Look, she can't afford to make it public that she intended to take a stripper to bed, any more than you can afford to be caught impersonating a stripper. She might kick you in the balls, but that won't damage your career as a lawyer, though maybe your career as a stripper." He chuckled.

Maybe Nelson was right, maybe it would take something wild and crazy to get her attention. And Tyler definitely wanted her attention—which was a new situation for him.

Tyler looked back into the room where another one of the women gave out a gasping scream as The Bandit grabbed and fondled her breast through her dress.

"Technically, he's not supposed to touch them."

"He's definitely gonna touch her if you don't do something about it. She has that predatory look."

Tyler turned to Nelson. "Can you catch this guy when he goes to the bathroom? Offer him a thousand dollars for the getup."

"A thousand? Man, are you crazy?"

Tyler just looked at him.

"Yeah, I guess you are, and at least you're good for it." Nelson put a hand on Tyler's shoulder. "In the meantime, keep both Sheila and Peggy warm for me."

Tyler grimaced. "I only agreed to come along with Sheila so I could get close to Tina. Guess that makes me a louse."

Nelson smiled. "Makes you human, man, but it's my guess Tina intends to take the stripper to her room tonight, and the only reason she's sticking around is to flaunt what she's got lined up for the evening. If you're flaunting, too, it's going to get very interesting."

Tyler tightened his hand on the balcony rail, which felt very solid beneath his fingers, an anchor of sorts. "You know this is crazy, don't you? I've never done anything this crazy, even in college."

"You only live once, so a little crazy isn't a bad thing."

Tyler reluctantly let go of the rail, and then made his way back inside through the crush of people to Sheila, who immediately draped herself over him. Absently, he ran his hand down the silky smooth skin of her bare leg. If he'd been interested, the dress she had on would have made for excellent access, and because he was accustomed to taking advantage of such access, his fingers crept under the hem.

When he looked across the room Tina had moved in closer to the stripper. Her expression was hard, as if she'd caught his move on Sheila.

Could Nelson be right? Could Tina be just a little jealous? Tyler's naughty fingers slid deeper under Sheila's dress. For the first time in the evening he was aroused and Sheila obligingly rubbed up against him as she leaned in to whisper intimately in his ear.

Tyler didn't have a clue as to what Sheila said to him. She was just like all the other women in his life. They'd take one look at him and his bank book and they'd trip all over themselves to get to him. It didn't feel real, and it certainly wasn't a challenge.

As far as he was concerned, Tina was the only woman in the room worth going for. Practically grinding his teeth, he watched her sliding bills in the stripper's thong with bold, seductive moves, unabashedly stroking the man. And the stripper enjoyed her attention.

Why not? Tina's tall figure might not be generous but she was perfectly proportioned, graceful and charismatic. Her straight hair complimented that narrow face, and she had those gorgeous changeable hazel eyes. When he'd made love to her, those eyes had gone a soft golden color that he desperately wanted to see again.

If he had any doubts about his plan to get Tina, now was the time to give them up. The Bandit was going to have Tina tonight over Tyler's dead body. No one knew anything about the man. He might harm her, or worse, he might please her.

Tyler intended to touch and caress Tina until she begged, and then possess her fully, if only for one more night. He doubted Tina would ever commit to anyone—she'd come out and told him that she wasn't interested. He wasn't supposed to be hurt because she didn't do relationships. It had been fun: the cruise, the fling afterward, a short-term romance. She'd laid it all out for him, explaining patiently that she didn't want more. That she needed nothing from him or anyone else.

It only made him crazy wondering. Why was she so independent? And why, when he'd already scored with her, did he still dream about her? He hadn't actually had sex with a woman since he'd been with Tina that last night at her home. She'd wound herself around him all night long, and then woken him up with a cup of coffee and a boot out the door. Later, she'd explained why she preferred not to see him again. Logically. Coolly.

It only made him burn.

So what would she think about a man crazy enough about her to do something really desperate? Tyler wondered bleakly. Would she be cool or could he make *her* burn?

"DOES OUR Bandit need a ride home?" The female voice drifted through the closed restroom door as Tyler awkwardly buckled the last piece of the loin plate into place.

"That's probably Lindsay. She must have dropped almost a hundred trying to get a hold of my cock." The stripper chuckled softly as he tucked his T-shirt into his jeans. Tyler thought he would probably be a huge disappointment to his audience if they could see him now. He looked just like a regular guy.

"I'll be walking him out."

This time it was Tina's voice. She sounded as if she hired a stripper every night of the week, and it made Tyler wince as he adjusted his newly acquired faux fur.

"Good for you."

Lindsay again, dripping venom.

The Bandit picked his head up. "Wow, Lindsay sounds lethal. You might have to rescue your lady." The guy stuffed Nelson's money carelessly into his pocket.

"Believe me, Tina can handle herself."

"I don't know, that lady, Lindsay, sounds like she wants to walk all over someone in those tiny little heel and leave a trail of bloody gouge marks behind. It would be an awesome cat fight. Too bad you paid me to get lost."

"I'm glad you remember. Can you wait here for at least fifteen minutes?"

"Sure, man, good luck. Just remember to grind it." The stripper thrust his hips forward. "That's the secret to success."

Tyler tried moving in the leather, and the chains

clinked all over his body. He felt as if he were going into an ancient battle. The Bandit had put the whole costume he'd stripped off during the show, including the mask and loin plate, on Tyler. The fur draped over his shoulders helped to hide the difference in his skin tone.

"There are some toys in the bag."

"Toys?"

"Some chains, cuffs, a blindfold. There are some whips and more leather. A decent piece of fur. Some ladies get off on the fur, some on the pain." He shrugged. "You never know."

"Sounds like you've moonlighted before."

The stripper held his hands out. "Hey, it's my job to please the ladies."

"And you take your job seriously." Tyler looked into the mirror. He didn't look like a bandit; the fur made him look more like a Neanderthal.

He grimaced. Could this possibly work? Or would Tina take one look at him and laugh in his face?

He'd better see if he could grind it. He thrust his hips forward and the ridiculous loin plate exaggerated his movements.

The stripper nodded. "Not bad. You're buff enough. Good abs. Just try to tilt your pelvis towards the ceiling."

He tried again. *I hope I don't throw my back out again.* Because of his old football injury, he sometimes had trouble with the muscles in his lower back.

But this time it would be worth it. Better than winning the homecoming game, better than anything.

"That's perfect." The stripper adjusted a few of the straps and then tucked things in. "Now you're all set."

"Thanks for your help."

"No problem. I made a fortune tonight."

Tyler took a deep breath and he opened the door. Tina stood directly outside. Her face was flushed, and she leaned forward on the balls of her feet as if anticipating...something more than she should have expected when hiring a stripper.

She smiled a slow, intimate smile. "Wow, you look so primitive." It came out like a purr. "I thought you might have gotten more comfortable. Taken something off..."

"I didn't think that's what you had in mind," he said deeply, suggestively. His *loins* swelled. He couldn't seem to help it.

Tina's baser instincts appeared to be fully engaged, and he planned to fully enjoy them.

Or was it the alcohol?

Why did he care? Suddenly he felt as primitive as he looked. He'd taken matters into his own hands, and all he wanted was to throw her over his shoulder and give her everything she appeared to want from him.

"You took so long and I'm so...ready," she breathed.

Tyler sucked in a breath at the sight of those heavy eyes and slick mouth. Her nipples stood at attention, and he had to clench his hands to keep from reaching out and touching her.

"Lead the way." Fortunately, the stripper hadn't spoken in a normal voice during the show. His deep tones had obviously been for effect. Tyler just hoped Tina was too drunk to notice the difference.

"My pleasure." She took his arm and led him to the elevators, leaning heavily on him.

He should have felt stupid dressed as a Neanderthal, but Tina's reaction had him getting into the part, especially when the elevator doors closed, and she boldly reached around him to pat his ass and then squeeze his buns.

"You're so deliciously tight back there. You must work out all the time." She pressed her hips against his. "I thought we might have a little workout session of our own before you go home."

"I don't mind getting a little physical after a performance." He couldn't resist. He ran his fingers over her collarbones, slipping down over her breasts, sliding over silk, and her erect nipples, mesmerized by the glow of desire in those golden eyes. "Especially with such an exceptionally beautiful woman."

"Ohhhh, that feels so good."

"Yes, it does." His voice sounded guttural but it wasn't an affectation.

"You have such beautiful blue eyes," she murmured.

"Thank you."

"Were they blue—" she gestured, and almost lost her balance "—before?"

Tyler steadied her. He didn't panic, though he hadn't even noticed the color of the stripper's eyes. Instead, he improvised. "Naw, they're contacts. I just put them in now. I didn't have time to do it before the performance."

Tina's brow furrowed.

He resisted the urge to kiss her. But mouth-kissing protocol might be different for strippers; besides, she'd probably recognize him if he kissed her.

"I like your eyes blue. But what's your real eye color?"

She had a death grip on the strip of fur around his neck.

"Kinda hazel, I guess. These contacts were worth the money if they turn you on." His hands came around to lift and caress her breasts.

Tina sucked in a breath. "I've never done this before, but I promise to pay you enough to make this worth it."

"Honey, anything you pay would just be icing on the cake. You feel so delicious." He thought about what he'd say if she offered to pay, and despite his pride he knew she'd be suspicious if he turned down the money cold.

"Hmmm. You certainly know where to touch a girl."

Tyler could feel her flesh swelling in anticipation of his touch, and he knew from past experience that she had on a skimpy little thong under that skirt that molded around her ass so lovingly.

The elevator dinged. And he nudged her shoulder. "Ladies first. Which room?"

"Sixteen."

Tina listed against him so he guided her down the hallway.

It seemed to take forever to reach the door. Then she handed him the key card to the room. He bent down and when her fingers slipped down toward the loin plate, he almost groaned aloud anticipating her touch.

When the door was finally standing open, he

dropped his leather bag of tricks. Then he looked down the hallway, first to the right and then the left.

Tina smiled her siren's smile from where she leaned against the wall, unsteady and obviously excited. She ran her wicked fingers leisurely up his naked thigh.

She whispered, "Don't worry, no one's going to see us, and I really want you." She traced where her necklace dipped down between her visibly sensitized breasts. "I *really* want you. And it's more than making Tyler pay for bringing that cow Sheila to the party."

Tina couldn't believe she'd said that, or thought it. When had she ever felt jealous of Tyler or any man? Jealousy was an emotion she couldn't afford. It meant you felt something more than just desire. It led to stupid things like commitments, which never lasted. Lives that became flat and defeating. She could feel her desire fizzling, as it had with other men in the past few months. She hadn't even told Emma about her forced celibacy. "Maybe this isn't a good idea."

Suddenly, The Bandit's strong hands came around her, pinning her up against the door by her shoulders. Tina barely had time to register that her feet were dangling above the floor, when he ground the leather loin plate against her hips. She automatically opened her legs to let him apply pressure where she most needed it, moaning with the pleasure of it.

Would he simply take her? Was that what she needed?

He leaned in, his breath was warm on her face, and she lifted her mouth to kiss him. The mask would make a kiss feel strange and exciting.

Instead of kissing her, he buried his face in her neck. "You feel so good, my little warrior."

The endearment was so much better than the insipid *princess* that The Bandit had called her when he'd met her in the lobby before the party. It had her biting him gently on the shoulder, careful not to draw blood. But she was beginning to feel hungry again. The juices were definitely flowing this time, and she knew her desire wouldn't stall, not if he continued to touch her like that under her linen skirt.

It was probably better that he didn't seem to want to kiss her. *Remember, he's a stripper. It's his job to turn you on, and make you crazy. It's just a bonus that he's gonna cure what ails you.*

Her body certainly remembered he was a stripper— a very hot one. She thought she might come right here up against the wall. Why didn't they just go inside, and get this over with? She was so ready.

But the sound of the elevator had him easing her back to the ground. She grabbed the doorframe in order to stay on her feet. Was it the alcohol or The Bandit that made her legs wobble? He grinned at her, all gorgeous teeth under the mask. Had his teeth been that nice before?

She lost her train of thought as an older couple went by with their bags in tow. They both looked shocked. Tina couldn't help herself; feeling naughty, she winked at them. The Bandit nodded like a gentleman, and then pushed Tina into the room roughly enough to raise her temperature. He shut the door behind them with an echoing thud.

"I think we shocked them. They might have had heart attacks right in the hallway," Tina said, laughing.

He didn't say a word; he just picked Tina up, and threw her over his shoulder like a caveman. Her purse dangled a minute before she dropped it on the floor.

"Hey," she laughed, pounding on his back. "With all of those muscles, you'd think you could be more of a gentleman in how you sweep me off my foot, feet." It should have embarrassed her—she was usually articulate. But, hey, he was going to get paid to have sex with her no matter that the most articulate lawyer in town was sloppy drunk. Or was it the adventure that had her so giddy?

"Probably drunk," she said aloud.

"Sweeping you off your feet is for the good guys. I'm just going to tie you up, strip off your clothes, and then I'm going to push myself into you until you scream for mercy."

His voice was gravelly, and she couldn't remember if he'd spoken like that earlier. Maybe it was for her benefit. But his words made her shiver with anticipation. "It definitely works for me."

He practically threw her down on the bed, and then stood over her. "Do you want something from the bar?"

She raised her arms above her head. "No, I've had enough, and I have to remember enough to tell the girls if it's padding in your pants or the real thing. I'm hoping it's the real thing." She lazily plucked at her nipple through her three-hundred-dollar shirt. Then, remembering, she took two folded bills out of the pocket of her skirt. She handed them to him, hardly believing she was desperate enough to pay to get out of this rut. What the heck was wrong with her? She fought her way up from the bottom of the food chain and she wasn't going to let a man interfere with her life now. Even if she had to pay for it from now on. "You'd better be worth it."

"Bitch."

"Yeah. That's what they call me behind my back. They call me The Shark to my face. I'm a hell of a hard-ass in the courtroom, and off…I…mean…out."

He hardly looked at the money. He looked directly at her, hungrily. He absently took the bills and put them in his bag. Then he dropped the bag on the ground as if it meant nothing.

"Sit up," he demanded.

"Huh?"

"You ready for sleep or you want to play?" He reached down to unbuckle one of the leather straps wrapped tightly around his waist.

She sat up on the end of the bed. "I definitely want to play."

"Unbutton the shirt or I'll rip it off."

Tina hesitated a second; ripping it off sounded sexy but practicality forced her to strip off her shirt. She hadn't always had nice things to wear.

She told herself the sexy little bra she had on underneath, hardly more than a scoop of nylon cupping her breasts, would certainly turn him on.

He knelt, the leather in his hands.

Tina pulled back a little. "I'm not into pain." She stated emphatically.

"I won't hurt you."

Did he sound familiar? Hadn't she heard that voice say those words before? But before she could concentrate he sucked her nipple right out of the nylon cup, and into his warm wet mouth, deeply into his mouth.

It was just a tiny bit forceful, almost too intense, but she didn't want him to quit. No, she leaned into him, putting a hand on each of those buff arms. "Ahh, that feels so good," she told him.

He laved her nipple, and then reached around her to release the hook on her bra with one expert flick. "I guess you do this all of the time." Did she sound disappointed? What was wrong with having an experienced man? Just because she had never paid for sex didn't mean it wouldn't be wonderful.

"I only want you. I can only think of you."

He sounded so sincere. Tina rubbed her fingers together as he removed her bra, and then threw it on the floor. Then he took the leather belt and fastened it around her breasts with the buckle in the back.

Tina looked down in surprise. The leather didn't exactly cover her breasts: they overflowed the leather binding above and underneath, her nipples resting on top like little cherries.

"You're beautiful." He ran his fingers back and forth over the leather and her tender flesh.

Tina moaned. Leather *was* sexy. Her breasts bulged

and the pressure felt amazing. "More," she whispered. "I want more of the leather."

His smile was feral under the mask. "My pleasure."

Taking off a thin, braided piece wrapped around his forearm, he looked at her with a wicked light in his eyes. "You sure you aren't into pain? I could whip you with this strap until you offer me everything I want from you."

The hard-ass of the courtroom could feel her eyes widening as she wondered if he really meant it. She shook her head emphatically.

The moment he hesitated felt like a lifetime.

Next he took the strap, and then wrapped it around her waist, tightly, and then knotted it where the leather got thin. The strap was tight sitting up against her belly button.

Tina sat up and looked down. It might have seemed silly but the leather looked sexy nipping in her waist and making her feel like a warrior woman from one of those ridiculous TV shows.

"More."

His hands spanned her waist, and then traveled up to her breasts to caress her until she didn't know if she wanted to bother with the leather she was so aroused.

He broke away from her, taking off his armbands one by one.

Tina ran her hands over the firm flesh of his arms. Up close he was just as buff as she remembered, but different somehow. Maybe it was the alcohol or his nearness that had her mind all fuzzy and other parts of her buzzing.

The Bandit fastened his leather cuffs to her ankles, leaving her Manolos in place.

"What are you going to do with these?" She turned her feet this way and then that way to admire how the cuffs looked with her shoes. They were the strangest, yet sexiest, accessories she'd ever worn with high heels.

Yes, everything about this turned her on.

Casually he produced a length of chain from the bag, tossing the length of it onto the floor and examining it before attaching it to one of the cuffs.

Tina gasped. She hadn't really noticed the ring on the leather cuff.

He winked as if he were immensely pleased with himself.

She felt it kick her in the stomach. Those eyes, that cute little wink, they had such an effect on her. They reminded her... No. It just felt this good because she was so into this fantasy.

A few feet across from the foot of the bed was one of those standard wooden desks with literature about the hotel and the room service menu. The stripper ran the chain around one leg of the desk, and then brought it back so he could attach it to the cuff on her other ankle. Tina picked up her legs, which were now adorned with cuffs and chains that loosely bound her to a desk. It was definitely a novelty.

Experimentally, Tina pulled on the cuffs. The desk was either really heavy or it was bolted to the wall because it didn't feel as if it might give way.

She was bound by more than just fantasy now. And it gave her a thrill.

Especially when he stepped over the thin chain and stood between her legs like he'd just conquered her.

She lifted her fitted linen skirt up over her hips to bunch up against the leather strand at her waist. Bare except for her thong, she pleaded, "Please." She ran her fingers over the silk of her thong, touching her dampened, hungry flesh.

He gazed down at her, his arousal pushing on the plate between his legs. Tina was betting it was all man in there, not any sort of lining or stuffing.

She ached to get a hold of the hard length of him.

Then he took off the tightest belt, the thick one that made his waist look so sexy.

Briefly, Tina wondered what he meant to do with it.

Without warning, he pulled her to her knees on the bed, chains jingling, and then jerked the thong from her hips.

She gasped in surprise.

When she was bare he threaded the leather between her legs. The strap was wide, and he eased her down until she was riding it. Then there was the most delicious pressure between her legs. Her knees wobbled, and she almost collapsed on the bed but he held her, keeping just enough pressure on the leather.

"How does that feel?" he asked.

"Oh, it feels so incredible." She rubbed against the leather, back and forth. Unexpectedly, an explosive orgasm suddenly tore through her, leaving her almost breathless. "I'm getting your leather all wet," she protested weakly.

He pushed her to the edge of the bed, sat her down with the strap between her legs and then knelt in front of her. "I'll just have to clean it up." He kept pressure on the leather, but he shifted it enough to tease her flesh on both sides with his tongue. It was like the leather band holding her breasts—her female flesh bulged out, pink and glistening.

In a moment he had her moaning and writhing beneath his tongue. "Oh, that's amazing," she cried as she shuddered with yet another incredible orgasm.

In a few minutes she was back, and this time she needed to touch him. She reached for him, and he stood stoically while she undid the buckle holding the pelvic plate in place. It was all him behind the loin plate. And he was so hard. When she got everything off, only a silky black thong lay between her hand and his swollen flesh. Lovingly she ran her fingers over his penis through the material.

He let go of the leather between her legs. "Close your eyes."

"Just take me," she begged. "No more games—I can't take it."

"Close your eyes and I'll give you everything you need."

She closed her eyes.

He lifted her head, and she felt him place a soft piece of leather over her eyes.

A blindfold. She couldn't see anything. It definitely fed her fantasy but...

"I want to see you. Remember, I'm supposed to give out all of the details," she protested.

He put her hands on his naked penis. "Feel me."

She did, running her fingers over the hot length of him, writhing as he slid his fingers down between her legs. The chains made a slight noise when her legs trembled. It reminded her that she was lying there chained *and* blindfolded. She wanted to rub her legs together. She wanted him to put out the fire he'd created. Just one hard thrust.

"Please," she breathed in the dark.

She heard him open a condom package, and in a moment he'd pushed her flat on her back on the bed.

"Thank you." In her rush to have him she'd forgotten everything else.

He went down on her first; she could feel it, the hard, smooth surface of his teeth, the softness of his lips, and finally his tongue on her clitoris. She arched, gasping.

Then he left her. She bit her lip rather than beg him to come back. But she ached for him. It had never been this intense.

He touched her with the fur, rubbing it over her throat, down over her nipples.

Then the fur feathered softly over her abdomen. She held her breath.

Finally he swept the fur between her thighs. Her sigh was as soft as the fleece. At the same time his strong fingers explored, almost roughly, seeking the core of her. The contrast overwhelmed her.

She shuddered, so close to an unfamiliar edge.

Abruptly he pinned her to the bed with all of his weight, thrusting his penis inside her in one stunning stroke.

And then he pulled out. "Do you want this? Me?"

She arched up. "Yes!"

Still he held himself over her. She could feel that he was holding something back.

It didn't matter. All she wanted was the release he could give her. Life should always feel this incredible.

"Please, Bandit, now. I'll give you a tip. A bigger tip."

"Are you begging?"

"Yes!"

"Don't forget. You begged me."

She made an angry, frustrated sound and tried to reach up and bite his neck. How could he make her feel so aroused, and then play games with her? "You bastard. Do what I bought you to do!"

He didn't complain. Instead he laughed softly. With a shift of his hips he entered her again, slowly, and then harder. Plundering her. Sobbing, she wound her arms around his neck. Through the roar of pleasure, the clinking of the chains and the sweat from the leather blindfold, she could only imagine those heavenly blue eyes glinting with holy hell as he took her to heaven.

2

TINA WOKE TO FIND a hairy arm flung across the pillow. She blinked at it. Her head hurt and her mouth tasted like sour milk, indicating she'd had a little too much to drink. She remembered indulging every time Tyler had put his hand up Sheila's skirt. Tina gritted her teeth. Why did she allow that man to get under her skin as easily as he'd gotten under Sheila's skirt?

And who was the man lying beside her?

Slowly the details came into focus. This man must be The Bandit stripper. The one who'd given her so many orgasms she'd lost count. Of course, she'd been too drunk to count. Hadn't she? It had to be the alcohol that had made her feel so giddy.

I can't wait to tell that idiot MD that I was right. I wasn't depressed. I just needed a change of male scenery.

She knew some people actually needed chemical help, but she wasn't one of them. In her case it was more a mind-over-matter thing, as she'd recently explained to her doctor.

The stripper made a little snorting sound that interrupted her train of thought.

Why hadn't he gone away?

Surely, strippers knew the protocol; even casual dates knew when to scoot out of a woman's room. Tina herself always left the man's house in the middle of the night to avoid those awkward mornings. The one time she'd brought a man home had been a mistake. She'd spent the next evening at Emma's doing a silly thing Emma called *a cry movie,* and pigging out on Chinese food.

The hairy arm moved.

Tina had to admit she was at a loss and it was a rare thing for her. What to do with a stripper who'd over-stayed his welcome? She'd certainly paid him enough. Even for all of those orgasms. But he was wonderful in the sack. Did she really want to get rid of him?

Maybe she could play nice and keep this particular option open. Seeing him had definitely been the best sort of therapy. And it would be cheaper than a shrink, the other option her MD had recommended.

She could probably even deduct him from her taxes for services rendered.

The other arm came up to drape around her shoulders. Tina should have felt claustrophobic. Hugging was foreign to her—an activity she avoided at all costs. Perhaps it was a postcoital connection or pre-coital possibilities that made this hug feel acceptable, but she couldn't just lie here and accept an invasion of her privacy.

Remember to be nice. But, she fully intended to take charge here. After all, this was her hotel room and passive wasn't her style.

She didn't passively accept anything. When she'd become an orphan and then a ward of the state at a tender age, she'd quickly learned that she had to fight for every little thing. Since then, she'd had this need to be in control. She thought of it as being the driver rather than the passenger. She just liked to drive.

She *always* drove.

"Do you mind moving your arm so I can get up?" Her tone was deadpan dry. *But nice.*

There was a moan from down inside the pillows.

"I don't know what your problem is, since I'm the one who had too much to drink."

Be sympathetic. Remember that you definitely want him again and again.

Another moan. However, it didn't invoke any sympathy.

Rather annoyed, Tina told him, "Really, this is just silly. You're a professional and you should have gotten out of here at a reasonable time instead of causing this awkward scene...." She softened her tone. "I definitely would have called you, or rather I would have called the service."

She tried to stretch and became aware that at some point she'd been freed from the ankle cuffs. Then she became even more aware that her bladder was under more pressure than was comfortable. Still, she didn't want to totally blow it. "I guess I could allow you to make it up to me. I haven't exactly been myself since this dumb cruise I took in the spring, and you've definitely cured what ailed me."

Maybe she sounded a little peevish, but she really needed to use the bathroom and grab a double espresso. Struggling against the weight of the arm wasn't enjoyable.

Was she nuts to also feel like it was kind of cozy under the warmth of his arm?

Of course not. She wasn't the cozy type any more than the hugging type. It must be the hangover.

"Please get up. This is getting embarrassing."

"Just give me a second." The voice sounded muffled but familiar.

Of course it was familiar—she'd just been intimate with the man. "I've given you more than a minute and I'm running out of patience." There, she'd used her cutting courtroom voice. It should have him out of here in minutes. She hadn't been christened *The Shark* for nothing.

The hand slid up her arm, intimately, seeking. It felt good, which angered her, so she reached over to push it away. Then she struggled out from under the dead weight until she came to the edge of the bed, where for some inexplicable reason, she hesitated.

She was naked.

She needed cover. The sheet and thin blanket were tangled around at least six feet of male flesh. The bedspread wasn't an option, as it was probably gross from the hundreds of guests who stayed in this hotel. She had no robe, because she liked to be naked, and she was usually totally comfortable with her body. Yet she hesitated to get out of the bed.

Why? Why should this time be any different? Maybe it was the paid part of the situation that bothered her, since she'd never paid for sex before.

"Why should I have to get up when technically this is my bed bought and paid for?" she mused aloud.

"Because I seem to have thrown out my back."

She looked over at him. With the mask gone and those incredible blue eyes blinking at her, there was no denying she'd seen that face before. "Tyler?" Her voice went shrill. "What the hell are you doing in my bed?"

Still lying on his stomach, he rubbed his hand over his beard-stubbled gorgeous face. "You hired me."

"I did no such thing. I hired The Bandit." She clung to the corner of the sheet as if it were a lifeline because her heart was sinking fast.

"You can negotiate for a refund, but I counted your orgasms last night, and I'm pretty sure you got your money's worth." He sounded so very smug.

"Get up. Get out. Just get." Her voice rose with every *get*. Her heart was not sinking. She was just disappointed in Tyler for lying so spectacularly to her. And she was angry. Very angry, she told herself.

Okay, why wasn't she furious?

"I can't. I've thrown my back out."

She scooted off the bed. It seemed safer to be naked and exposed than to be close to *Tyler.* "What exactly does that mean?" she asked scathingly.

"I'm having muscle spasms in my back, probably from our workout last night. I'll be okay if you'll soak a towel in hot water and lay it on my back.

Eventually the muscles will loosen up, and I'll be able to get up."

"Our workout? It wasn't even supposed to be *you* last night. And I will not soak a towel and put it on your back. I'm never touching you again. You...you, low-life probationer!"

"Okay, then just leave me. I'll call down to the desk for some anti-inflammatory medication. I'll request a later checkout, take a nap, and in a few hours I'll be just fine." He flexed his shoulders, and then with a grimace stopped trying to shift.

He looks like a fish floundering.

Offering him no sympathy, Tina looked around for her clothing. It was strewn around the room with an abandon that made her grind her teeth. "Technically, this is my hotel room."

True, she hadn't even brought in her overnight bag from the car—she'd barely had time to tuck her tooth-brush into her purse because of some last-minute dinner glitch—but it was the principle of the thing.

"I'll be happy to reimburse you the cost of the room," he said so reasonably Tina just exploded.

"And what about the cost of our little interlude? What the hell did you think you were doing pretending to be a stripper?"

He started to shrug, and then tensed up again. The pain on his face stood out in stark relief, and for a moment she almost felt sorry for him.

"I'm not sure I knew what I was doing. All I could think about was that I didn't want him to touch you. I'm sorry if I've caused you any embarrassment. But hey, I saved you from a stripper. Who knows where the man's been or whether he even intended to use a condom!"

"I brought plenty of condoms!"

"You were too far gone to tell if he even used one or not."

"I was not. I was in control. In fact I remember every detail...." She trailed off. The blush started at her forehead and seemed to travel down her body. She did remember every detail, and it had been incredible. And it had been Tyler.

She swallowed hard.

Tyler, who strode into a courtroom with the careless elegance of a 1940s actor. Tyler, with dark blond hair still streaked from the cruise, since he wore it just a little longer than was absolutely professional. Tyler, with eyes so intensely blue they warmed like a summer sky, which had his witnesses, both male and female, stammering to please during their testimonies.

He simply had that effect on people.

And that body. He'd sculpted it even more since the last time they'd made love. Tyler was so perfect, he was scary.

Not scary.

She was never scared.

And she just didn't do relationships, even with perfect men.

Perfect? What was she thinking? He was just like every other man in the world, telling lies to get what he wanted. She couldn't trust him!

"How could you?" she raged. "After I told you that I didn't want to see you again? I think I was rather explicit after you stayed at my place. What part of *never again* didn't you understand?"

She took a breath and then it hit her. She even pointed a finger at him. "And you had your hand up Sheila's skirt last night. If you ever touch me again, I'm going to fillet you!"

Did he smile? Had he dared to smile? She would teach him while she had him at her mercy. Her own smile felt feral.

"You don't mean that. You're just angry." His eyes were earnest. "You haven't even given us a chance."

"We were together on the cruise."

"That wasn't reality. It was a singles' cruise. We have a lot in common in real life."

"And we had a few dates after that, but you're a lawyer, how many times do I have to tell you that I don't date lawyers!"

"More times."

She wanted to stomp her foot or throw something at him. "How many more times?"

"A lot more times."

"Get up and get out!" She pointed at the door.

"No can do, unless you intend to help me out." He sounded so matter-of-fact.

She cautioned herself to be calm, like him. This was no time to let her emotions rule her. "You need a hot towel placed on your back to loosen up the muscles? And then you'll be able to get dressed and leave the room? I want to be very clear on what I need to do to get rid of you."

"Some anti-inflammatory medicine would help if you have anything on you."

"Massage therapist? Dancing girls? An eight-course meal brought in and fed to you with an after-dinner mint placed on the pillow?"

"I know, it's a pain. This hardly ever happens anymore since I started strength training for my back. I probably shouldn't have picked you up."

"You call slinging me over your shoulder picking me up?" She laughed tauntingly. "Well, let me tell you, it's hardly romantic, so you won't have to do it again."

"Don't lie. You loved it. You were so hot I thought the sheets would catch fire."

She pushed her hair back. How to argue when he was absolutely right? "I can't help it if you're such a loser you can't lift your lover." It sounded lame but it should at least put a dent in his ego.

"I'll work up to the lifting part," he offered.

"No way in hell. I'm not your lover anyway." She stalked over to pick up her purse from where she'd dropped it on the floor, and then came back to sit on the edge of the bed while she rummaged through it. "I've got to have some anti-inflammatory in my purse."

"Great."

"Then you don't need the hot towel?" She knew she sounded hopeful, but the nurse thing just didn't appeal to her. There was no empathy in her soul, just impatience.

"I'll be able to move as soon as the medication

kicks in. I usually take the pills, and then I go back to sleep for an hour or so."

She turned around and stomped into the bathroom, naked and too angry to feel awkward. She grabbed a towel and put it in the tub and then she turned on the hot tap full force. "I can't believe this," she muttered. "I can't believe he lied to me. How could this have happened?" She watched the steam rise up from the running water with great satisfaction.

She'd sworn off Tyler after she'd been stupid enough to allow him to break her rule of no men at her home. Something about Tyler got under her skin. Well, she had no intention of dating a lawyer no matter how incredible the chemistry between them. The worst part was he seemed to want more than just sex.

Although the man was amazing at sex.

She wiped away the perspiration on her forehead from the steam rising up from the tub. The towel was going to melt if she didn't get it out—which suited her purpose perfectly. She turned off the tap.

She reached down to touch the steaming towel and then drew away. "Ow."

"Are you okay?"

"Just be quiet. Okay? I'm so angry with you right now. How dare you come back into my life when I specifically told you goodbye."

"Jeez, I'm sorry. I couldn't help it. I wanted you so badly I would have done anything to be the one you were looking at with that hunger on your face."

She dropped the towel back into the tub with a satisfying splat. "Have you no pride?" she yelled. "There you are, a successful lawyer. Every woman in the field is trying to snag you. Yet you've been reduced to saying silly, sappy things to a woman who's told you repeated times she doesn't want anything to do with you. I should sue you for harassment—and use Beaterman as my lawyer while I'm at it."

She managed to squeeze some of the excess water out of the towel by pressing the base of the bathroom trash can against the tub. Then she wrapped the towel in two other towels to avoid the prospect of the very hot water dripping on her naked body.

Guess it's a good thing I didn't bother to get dressed. And isn't he going to be hot under the collar when I put this burning hot towel on his back?

"Beaterman's an ass."

"That's exactly why I'd use him. He drives you crazy, and he'd bust your butt, just to impress me." She eyed the steam coming off the towel. "This is really, really hot," she warned him as she approached the bed.

"The hotter the better." He grimaced again.

She felt her conscience kicking in. Too bad, since she felt like kicking *him.*

"No, I mean, it's seriously hot." She turned around just short of the bed to take it back and rinse it in cold water.

"I can stand a little heat, which is exactly why I'm still interested in you. Even if everyone tells me you're a bitch. Even if they tell me you're not someone to snag or bag. Even when you snarl at me."

Tina turned around. Snarling.

"Well, you may have bagged me, but you certainly haven't snagged me." She leaned over the bed and dumped the hot towel directly on his back over the sheet.

Tyler made a sound, a cross between a moan and a grunt. He came up off the bed a few inches before falling back onto the bed. Those beautiful eyes actually rolled. "Damn. Damn. Damn!"

Were there tears in those incredible eyes or were they just watering? Tina didn't know, but she felt like a murderer.

She dumped the towels she'd used to transport the hot towel, then grabbed a bottle of water from the minibar, opened it and poured the entire thing over his back.

His long *ohhhhhh* of relief made her sink down on the edge of the bed, still naked, vulnerable and now feeling guilty as hell.

"My ass is getting all wet," she complained.

"So is mine," he choked out.

"This isn't going well."

"That's an understatement. I think you might have to call an ambulance—I think I've got second-degree burns."

Guilt flared, though she didn't let it show when she barked, "Let me see. You're probably just being a big baby." She pulled the wet sheet and sodden towel off his back. His skin was red under there, but she couldn't see any blisters. "I'm sure you'll feel fine after we rub some aloe vera on it."

"Rub?"

"Yeah. I've got some in my purse. I intended to

come early yesterday to lie by the pool, but there was a small crisis with the dinner, so I didn't get a chance."

"I don't think I trust you to rub anything on me. It will probably be pure alcohol, not aloe vera."

"I *do* have an entire minibar from which to choose my poison."

"You *are* nasty."

"A compliment. You must be cooling off."

"Is the towel still warm? Just put it on my lower back. No rubbing."

"I'll rub if I want to. But don't think that means I feel sorry for you. You're the one who deceived me. I do not feel guilty." She muttered the last part under her breath.

He moved his arm to get her attention. She placed the warm towel on his lower back and then risked a look into his face. "I'm sorry," she found herself saying.

Those blue eyes met hers with a look of total sincerity. "And I'm sorry I deceived you. It was impulsive and stupid, and I shouldn't have done it. But I'll never forget or regret it."

Tina's heart fluttered, a very uncomfortable sensation. She climbed off the bed to get the aloe vera out of her bag. "I won't forget it, either, and you definitely owe me two hundred bucks."

"Don't you think I was worth it, my little warrior?"

She bared her teeth. "Do you want me to dump a bottle of tequila on your back or the gel?" She held up the bottle but when she made eye contact she noticed he wasn't looking at the gel, but at her breasts. "Stop."

"I can't help it. Your breasts are so beautiful, so perfect."

"Just stop. I'm mad enough."

"You're not mad. You're confused and you hate the sensation."

"Get out of my head!" One of the things that bothered her about him was his ability to read her. He was a good lawyer, because he knew people. But she wasn't going to allow him to get to know her. She had all kinds of things to hide, from him, from herself.

"Leave it. Find another woman. They're falling all over themselves to get to you. Like Sheila."

"I don't want Sheila. I want to see you again." He cocked an eyebrow. "I figure you owe me after almost burning me to death."

"After what you did?"

"It was an excellent cause. Weren't you just a little bit afraid to go home with a stripper you knew nothing about?"

She rubbed her fingers together. "I didn't take him home. You know I never take anyone home."

"I meant to a hotel room." Those eyes smiled at her. "I know you don't take men home. It's what gives me hope."

"I'm not afraid."

"Sure."

She wanted to wipe the smug look off his face. "I'm not afraid of anything. I'm a modern woman who can choose whom she goes to bed with. And I had condoms. A whole bunch of condoms."

He looked her over. "You keep saying that, honey."

"Why? You can't do anything about it anyway."

"Maybe, maybe not. Why are you walking around naked? It's very callous of you."

"To remind you of what you're missing."

"Really?"

"No. I just didn't think it was a good idea to try to wring out hot towels in silk. Why should I mess up my clothes when you've already seen me in my skin?"

"It's gorgeous skin."

"Thank you."

With the gel in one hand, she crawled carefully over to him. He seemed harmless, although entirely attractive.

She didn't think she should straddle his waist. He'd probably cry if she did. Leaning over, she looked at his back. Still no blisters.

"I'm going to rub this gel on your back, so don't act like a baby."

"Just get it over with."

She squirted the gel in her hands, rubbed them together and then started on the top of his shoulders. His shoulders were broad and muscular, a nice even tan color. She massaged, getting into a rhythm.

"Hmm, that feels so good."

It did feel good. In fact, she'd scooted closer, her hip against his hip and hands flat on the muscular plains of his back. The puddle in the sheets didn't bother her as it still felt warm. "I'm glad it doesn't hurt," she said lazily.

"No. It feels so good I guess I'll have to tip *you*." Did he sound as if he were breathing harder?

She sucked in her own breath. Did he have to remind her of what they'd done last night, especially when she had him naked and under her hands? Her nipples tightened and tingled.

She rubbed her moist hands lower, and lower, to the indent of his waist. "The skin is a little red back here. Are you sure I'm not hurting you?"

"Honey, you're killing me." He shifted under her hands.

"I should have given you the anti-inflammatory first."

"This inflammation has nothing to do with my back muscles."

She laughed.

"Maybe you should stop. Just give me the anti-inflammatory, and I'll sleep it off." He sounded disgruntled.

"Are you uncomfortable, darling?"

"No, you witch."

"That's bitch to you." She felt so good. She wanted to touch him everywhere.

"Tickle me."

"What?"

"Distract me before I kill myself rolling over to put my hands on your delectable breasts."

She leaned down so her erect nipples grazed his skin through the thick, sticky gel. "How does that feel?"

"Don't tease."

"I can't help it." In fact she wasn't really teasing

anymore. "It feels so good." Her erect nipples grazed the hot spot on his back and slid in the sticky gel. Bending closer she rubbed them back and forth. The feeling radiated to lower parts. "Oh," she sighed.

"Tina, I regret that I can't do anything for you in this condition. Baby, I can't even see you." She felt the frustration in his tensed muscles and heard it in his voice.

"You can feel me." Without putting any of her weight on his sore back, she leaned even closer until her breasts were almost flattened against his flesh.

"Come over to my place tonight. We can soak in my hot tub. I'll make you feel so good. I promise. Please." He sounded desperate.

It was the desperation that made her think about what she was doing. Hadn't she meant to get rid of him? Permanently? She pulled back. "No."

"Why not?" He sounded even more frustrated now. "You obviously want me as much as I want you! Your tight little nipples are burning holes in my back. Let me take care of you. I promise to make you feel so good, honey."

"I'm not your honey."

"That's right. You preferred little warrior."

She got up and wiped her goopy hands on the blanket. "I might have thought it was cute in the moment."

"You melted for me."

"I melted for The Bandit." She put more of the bed between them.

"It was me and I can prove it."

"You won't have the chance."

"You're scared. But I'm going to teach you to trust me."

"Now that makes perfect sense." She tossed her hair over her shoulder and then realized she'd probably gotten some of the goop in her hair. "Damn. Now I've got this stuff in my hair."

He stretched cautiously. "The muscles feel looser. It must have been the massage."

"Good. Then there's no reason for me to stick around and babysit you."

"I want to see you tonight."

"There's no need. And besides, you're not going to want to put any strain on your back for a week or more. By then you'll have found another girl to bag." As she began to pull on her clothes, she purposely chose a spot in the room where he couldn't turn to look at her.

"You want me. But you're afraid."

She stopped with one foot out of her skirt and one foot inside of it. "I'm not afraid of anything."

"Then agree to a date."

"No." She managed to slip into the skirt without falling over. How dare he think she was afraid of him? He didn't have that much power over her. Once people had had power over her, and they'd abused it. That would never happen again.

"Then go out with me this weekend. Let me treat you to a harmless dinner."

"It's a waste of our time. I've told you so many times. I don't *do* lawyers."

"Honey, if you'd done me any more I wouldn't just be incapacitated, I'd be dead."

She grinned as she wiped her nipples with Kleenex and then buttoned her shirt up. She hadn't bothered with a bra and it was obvious. She felt just the tiniest bit sore, but so ready for him to touch her again. She ran her fingers over her nipples, imagining. "You'd better stay away or I might kill you."

"I'd die happy."

"And I'd go to prison for murder."

"Please, Tina. Prove to me that you're not afraid and that you really don't want me, and then I'll leave you alone."

She paused to rummage around in her purse for the anti-inflammatory. "You'd leave me alone if I can prove I don't want you?"

"Come where I can turn my head to see you. This is making me crazy."

"I'm dressing," she teased.

"You're lying. I heard every sound you made getting dressed. It's such a turn-on to hear you sliding into clothes you shed so gracefully."

"Stop it." But if he checked now, he'd find her hot and wet and very interested. "I'm not interested."

"I wish I could check."

How did he do that? It was as if he could climb into her thoughts. "What are you talking about?"

"Check to see if you're moist for me."

"How?" But she knew what he'd say. She wanted him to say it.

"Running my fingers over your clit then sliding them inside you so I can feel how wet and swollen you are."

She sat down on the bed because her legs suddenly felt unsteady. "At dinner?" The image came to her of him slipping his hand between her legs at Lagoona's restaurant while they dined. The snowy tablecloths would hide everything but the sensual expression on her face.

"Would you like that? Fine silver, tablecloths, and while you're sucking lobster out of the shell, my fingers are stroking your clit? I know you taste better than lobster."

How did the man read her fantasies?

"It's no big deal. I've done it before," she lied to him ever so casually. "The foreplay isn't as exciting as the lobster."

"Then do it for the lobster."

She fingered her nipples. She'd been petted in public but she had a feeling he'd make it memorable. "It sounds tempting. Call my secretary." She threw the travel-size package of anti-inflammatory on the bed, and then followed it up with a bottle of water that bounced off his shoulder to lie beside him. "I've really got to go. I've got better things to do."

But when the door closed behind her, she leaned against it on unsteady legs. In truth, she *didn't* have anything better to do and it scared her to the bone. But she had no intention of being available to Tyler no matter how tempting the lobster or his touch.

TYLER REACHED for the phone on the table by the bed, a painful endeavor. He pulled it close enough to dial the operator and then Nelson's number. "Hey, buddy, I need you to come and get me. I can hardly move."

He heard Nelson chuckle. "She hit you? What'd she use? A chair?"

"No, I threw my back out having the greatest sex of my life."

Nelson sounded satisfyingly stunned. "It didn't bother her that you impersonated her stripper last night? I thought you'd at least have a black eye or two."

"I don't think she would hit a guy who was already down. But she did try to burn me to death with a hot towel and then drown me."

"Sounds exciting. You get all of the interesting women. But this one—she's different. Maybe she got burned big-time by a sack-of-shit boyfriend. Do you want me to write you up a recommendation?"

"I don't think she'd believe any recommendations."

"It's sickening to have to admit, but you are a decent guy under all that male perfection. Your dogs like you, you visit your grandmother and occasionally you even do pizza night with your nieces. Of course, you make guys like me want to ralph, but what's she got against you?"

"I lied to her because my friend told me to."

"You should thank me. I just pushed you a little. I can't stand it when you're too perfect. What's the plan now?"

"Come and get me. I want out of here so I can go home, soak in the hot tub and then prepare for my next strategic move. She tentatively agreed to a date, but she has no intention of following through, so I've got to be creative and impress her."

"You still haven't gotten her out of your system?"

"No, the more I see the softer side of Tina, the more convinced I am that I want her."

"Burning you with a towel is soft?"

"No, it's not that. It's like she loses the attitude when we're intimate. It's hard to explain."

"I'll bet it's hard to explain—because you're suffering from temporary insanity, buddy. Obviously caused by an insufficient amount of sex."

"Nelson…"

"Okay. I'm coming, but I'm going to stop and get coffee. The pretty lady I enjoyed last night wore me out."

Tyler didn't know if Nelson was teasing or not because the man had a rough charm that managed to land him women with astonishing regularity. "You try exercising somewhere other than between the sheets."

"Why?" Nelson sounded honestly confounded.

"Are you coming or not?"

"Damn if you don't get yourself in the most interesting messes," Nelson groused.

"This one is your fault, buddy, so just get your butt down here and bail me out. Oh and thanks, Nelson. I owe you everything, man."

3

LOOKING ACROSS the aisle of the church at the tall, skinny boy who was supposed to escort her down the aisle at Emma's wedding rehearsal, Tina whined, "Emma, how could you? All of those gorgeous cousins and I get the adolescent with the acne and flaming red hair?"

"Stop complaining," Emma admonished.

Her friend's uncharacteristic response made Tina take a closer look at her. Emma seemed to be on the verge of tears.

"What's wrong? This is your dream moment, your dream man and your dream life." Did she sound cynical? She hoped not. *Although I'd surely cry if I were going to be stuck with one man for the rest of my life.*

"Everything's going wrong and I don't need you to add to the problem." The bride-to-be sniffed.

Looking over the wedding party lined up at the back of the church all ready for the rehearsal, Tina didn't see any catastrophe large enough to explain Emma's display of emotion. "What's wrong? Have you watched your cry movie lately?" Emma had a whacked-out theory that if she had a good cry over a sad movie on a regular basis, she would be better able to control her emotions at stressful times. The theory didn't appear to be working.

Emma sniffed louder.

Tina tried not to panic. She hated tears more than anything. In fact, the one time she'd attended one of Emma's cry movies, she'd actually cried for the first time in ten-plus years. It had been a horrifying experience. "Don't cry. Please. Aren't you supposed to be glowing or something?"

"That's pregnancy, not the wedding."

"What's wrong? Maybe we can fix it. Or is it just nerves?"

"Maybe," Emma choked out.

Tina rubbed her fingers together. "Good. Okay then. Shall we allow ourselves to be escorted down the aisle by these gorgeous gentlemen?" She smiled widely at the assembled cast, hoping they would be patient a moment longer.

Abruptly, Emma dissolved into tears and ran out the doors, stage left.

It felt almost surreal and everyone looked shocked, especially the groom-to-be.

Tina kept smiling. "Bridal nerves, nothing to be worried about. I'll just go and get her…." She held both her hands up in front of her to stop Tony as he appeared to want to bolt after his bride-to-be.

"I promise I'll bring her back in a minute." Tina hit the doors at a run despite her three-inch heels, and very tight suede pants. The Florida humidity hit her like a wall.

In the parking lot, Emma stood looking utterly bereft with her arms wrapped around her waist as if she were comforting herself. Right away, Tina knew she should have allowed Tony to be the one to follow Emma. He was probably better at the comforting thing. Tina decided to try to be matter-of-fact. Maybe it would help Emma regain her composure.

"This better be good. I'm going to melt like the Wicked Witch of the West in these pants—it's hot as Hades out here. I'm sorry I criticized your new nephew. I'll hold his arm, his hand, I'll even marry him if you'll smile and go inside. Because in a minute your hair is going to be a frizzy mess instead of looking gorgeous...."

Emma only cried harder.

"What is up?" Tina shifted from foot to foot. "You're scaring Tony."

More tears.

"Frankly, you're scaring me, too."

Looking up through troubled, gray-blue eyes, Emma confided, "I'm scared. What if I'm making a mistake? You're always telling me there's no such thing as long-term love. And then there's the fertility issue." Emma dissolved into hiccups.

Tina sagged. "We talked about this. With all the recent medical advances, you probably won't have the trouble your mother had getting pregnant. Even your ob-gyn reassured you. Then Tony told you it wasn't going to be an issue between you. He said he'd be happy to adopt."

The bride-to-be nodded.

"Which made me respect him," Tina said thoughtfully. "You know, you guys can probably make a go of it. Children. A long-term marriage. The whole enchilada…."

"That's not what you've been saying." Emma exploded into sobs that shook her slight frame. "You don't even believe in love."

Tina hovered, hands flapping uselessly at her sides.

Emma looked so forlorn, and Tina knew this was partially her fault for opening her big mouth.

So she found herself wanting to do more than just stand there while her best friend cried her heart out. *Doesn't she know I don't do this mushy stuff?*

Living with the Mrs. Grangers of the world hadn't taught Tina to conduct real relationships. And of course, she'd been stuck with Worst Foster Mother of the Year Mrs. Granger the longest. It was only at Emma's insistence that Tina had any sort of connections outside of work.

But Emma obviously needed some mushy stuff now. She took a step closer, and then buried her head in Tina's shoulder.

Ah, hell.

Tina awkwardly put both of her arms around Em. "You know this is crazy. You know you're going to be just fine. Why would you listen to me, anyway? You know I'm just a cynical bitch."

"You are not a bitch." Emma clung to Tina.

"You're just having a case of the jitters. It's anxiety."

Tina patted awkwardly, hoping she was getting this friend thing right and slightly amazed at how much it mattered to her.

Was that a watery smile? Tina hoped so. All the hugging was putting creases in her raw silk blouse. "Now, let's go in there so I can put my arms around something male, even if he is thirteen and looks like a matchstick."

Emma untangled her arms. The mulish look on her face said everything. "I want you to go in and get Tony for me."

Tina shook her head until her hair swung. "Tony already knows about your fertility worries. He already said it's okay. You can discuss it tonight after we get rid of all these people. It'll be fine. You'll see." Tina tugged on Emma's arm.

Emma smiled grimly and held her ground. "I want to talk to Tony."

Tony hit the door open as if on cue, and Tina took flight, trying to grab the door he'd just come through before it closed, but the tight pants slowed her progress even more than the heels.

They didn't need her as a witness. They didn't need her at all.

But the doors shut and locked in her face.

She turned around, debating whether or not it was worth ruining her six-hundred-dollar spike heels to avoid having to walk past the lovers on the narrow sidewalk.

She decided it was best to wait and see if Tony would prove an insensitive jerk, impatient with his bride for having a panic attack on the day of her rehearsal. This was just like Emma. She was too practical to have a panic attack on her actual wedding day when she could get it over with the day before the actual wedding.

Would he understand Emma's dilemma?

"What's wrong, sweetheart?"

His deep voice soothed, and his tender touch wiped away most of Emma's tears. Tina felt the casing around her heart cracking just a little. Could two committed people make a go of a relationship despite the ridiculous odds? Would someone ever look at her with such a loving expression?

I must need a drink. I've got wedding whimsy.

"I'm just worried about this infertility thing...." Emma's voice broke. "And I..."

Tony bent down and wrapped his arms around his bride-to-be.

Tina felt a bit like a voyeur who was watching all of her presumptions fly out the window. Tenderness and concern were most evident between the happy couple. Where was his anger at the interruption of the nuptial practice and his concern for his ego in front of his family?

Why wasn't Tony yelling?

He looked over at her, and Tina shrugged. Should she intervene?

"Don't look at her. She'll run first chance she gets and ruin her heels. That's the only reason she's still standing there, because she'd sink and get grass stains on her Choo shoes," Emma murmured.

Tina nodded emphatically.

"What's really wrong, *querida?*"

"I guess I'm scared. I just needed to have your arms around me for a minute."

The door bumped behind her. Tina leaned against it and said, loudly, "Hey, we're busy out here."

The pressure on the door stopped immediately.

"I love you so much and I want to marry you. Nothing else matters." Hitching up his trousers, Tony got down on one knee.

"Emma, will you please marry me tomorrow?"

"Yes," Emma burst out. "I'd even marry you tonight."

Tina sagged heavily against the doors. "Not tonight. Tonight is the preparty. We're supposed to live it up. Without pressure." They were going to make it. Tony and Emma were going to live happily ever after. At that moment, she would have bet her partnership on it. If she made partner.

When Tony got to his feet, Emma wrapped her arms around his neck and cried again…this time, healing tears.

I have to admit it makes me want to sniff a bit myself.

After some hugging and kissing that made Tina squirm, they went around to the front of the church along the sidewalk. They entered the building, and Tony escorted them down the aisle, which no longer seemed impossibly long.

Tina traversed the aisle the second time around with Mark, the skinny nephew, as if it were a journey she were taking: a journey of faith in her friend, faith in the ritual of marriage and faith in the future. For the moment, she believed.

Later, full of rehearsal cake and wine, Tina sat and visited with Emma. "This is very nice. I like the idea of a rehearsal party. If I ever planned to get married, maybe I'd have a rehearsal party and then skip out."

"With or without the groom?" Emma asked.

"Now that's a question." Tina nodded her head toward Emma. "But you don't have to worry anymore. No more stress. Tomorrow, you are going to have a beautiful wedding."

Emma smiled whimsically at her friend. She never expected to hear Tina say anything good about a wedding. "You sound kinda mellow. I think this wedding stuff is rubbing off on you."

Tina raised her wineglass as if giving a toast. "For a moment there, I actually felt sentimental."

"Miracles never cease."

"Don't count on any long-term effects. Remember, I never said whether I would skip out with the groom."

"I know, but someday you might surprise me." *And yourself.*

Tina clinked her glass against Emma's. "I seriously doubt it. Here's to *your* forever and *my* never."

"That sounds more like my Tina." Yet there was a flash of something vulnerable in Tina's eyes. Emma wondered if her friend did feel mellower about relationships, despite a childhood filled with dysfunctional strangers.

Yet that same past had instilled in Tina an empathy

that motivated her to devote some of her valuable time to the hurting women and children at the shelter. Emma thought Tina's pro-bono work was especially telling. It proved that somewhere under her tough exterior, Tina had a heart. And it seemed to be warming up.

"Can we please talk about something besides romance now?" Tina asked. "I've had my fill."

Totally willing to oblige her friend, because she'd been dying of curiosity, Emma leaned forward in a conspiratory fashion to ask, "Whatever happened with The Bandit stripper? Surely you came to your senses."

"I not only slept with him, I had the best sex of my life," Tina told her emphatically.

Emma could feel herself blush. Even when she'd been trying to explore and enhance her sexuality, she'd never imagined taking a stripper to bed. Curiosity got the better of her. "What was he like?"

"He was like a Neanderthal. He picked me up and tossed me onto the bed. Then he put those pieces of leather in sensitive and strategic spots. Next he tied me up and blindfolded me. It was rather amazing," Tina said in a rush.

Did Tina look less than her usual confident self? "Did he hurt you?" Emma asked. "Make you do something uncomfortable?"

"No, he was very considerate, for a lying jerk."

Emma sat back as casually as possible, but she took a healthy gulp of the wine. "What was the lie? Surely you didn't believe it would really all be him under that silly loin plate?"

"No, I believed it would be The Bandit underneath all of that leather. And it was Tyler."

"Tyler Walden?"

"The one and only."

Emma had to take another sip of wine to hide her incredulous smile.

This was priceless.

"How did Tyler end up as the stripper?"

Tina swirled the wine around and around in her glass.

Emma noticed again how Tina always fidgeted when she talked about Tyler. He'd somehow managed to breach Tina's formidable defenses, and it tickled Emma how persistent he was being. Tyler was an amazing man: a successful trial lawyer who kept the circuit buzzing with his bold style. Of course, he kept the heart of every woman buzzing with his careless, Redford-like elegance.

It gave her hope for her friend's future because this man could be worthy of Tina. He might even be able to keep up with her. But knowing Tina she might have killed off any opportunity to be with him. "What did you do to him? Can he still have children? Has he filed a lawsuit?"

The wineglass hit the table with a thump and splash. "I just burned him a little."

"Really gave him a piece of your mind, huh?"

"No, I literally burned his back with a hot towel."

Emma leaned forward. "I'm confused."

"No more than I. The man threw his back out and wanted a hot towel to loosen it up. I just obliged him."

"That's pretty low. So, how are you going to make it up to him?"

"Why would I do such a stupid thing? He's supposed to make it up to me—if I were going to have any more to do with him, which I'm not!"

"Why not? Was he a disappointment? Did you discover he was all…padding?"

"No. The man is well enough endowed," Tina admitted reluctantly.

"So he just doesn't know what to do with it?" Emma smiled, hoping Tina wouldn't comment on her blush.

"Cute. And bold. And you're blushing. But your point is going to be lost on me. So he's a good lover. But he's entirely too persistent. Clingy, even."

"Only good? No wonder you're not interested." The blush felt like a holdover from her previous, inhibited life. More true to her new self was that Emma was actually having fun goading her friend, watching her literally squirm.

Tina tapped the base of her wineglass on the tabletop. "So he's better than good."

"I thought he must be decent—after all, he wore you out enough that you let him sleep over."

"He didn't wear me out!"

"Oh, then why did you let him stay over?" Emma took a sip of her wine to hide her gloating smile.

"I don't know!" Tina sighed. "And I don't understand why he keeps coming back when I actually go out of my way to be bitchy to him." She waved her arms around.

Emma swallowed her smile at Tina's unexpectedly dramatic reaction. "What a surprise," she remarked drolly.

However, Tina was on a roll and didn't seem to notice her sarcasm. "The man's gorgeous and incredibly successful, so why can't he pick on some wide-eyed secretary, social worker, or a stenographer? Why does he continue to pester me when I've made it painfully clear I'm not interested? Is he into pain?"

"Did he have whips and chains in addition to the leather and fur?"

"Very funny. Although he did tie me up with a chain and blindfold me. It was amazing." Tina blinked owlishly, as if she still couldn't believe it.

Emma didn't think it had anything to do with the wine. For once, a man had gotten under Tina's very thick skin. "Maybe he found it amazing, as well. Apparently, you're unforgettable." And she meant it. Tina commanded attention by just strolling into a room. But underneath her confidence, there was a hint of insecurity. Tina seemed almost frightened by any hint of the softer emotions, by tenderness, or tears.

And lately, Emma had come to understand that Tina was afraid of anything that even smelled like a commitment. So perhaps if she was reassured that she could handle it, Tyler might have an opportunity to worm his way deeper into her defenses before she even realized what was happening. "Maybe you shouldn't take him so seriously. Just keep him around for laughs. It sounds like The Bandit thing was fun." Emma kept her voice casual so as not to scare Tina off.

"He did offer to make up for his deception with a lobster dinner." Tina wouldn't make eye contact. Instead, she smoothed out the wrinkle in the table-cloth in front of her.

"That sounds promising. You love lobster."

"We both know it's just a bribe."

"So? You use bribery and negotiation all the time. Only this time it'll be fun. Make him follow up the main course with intercourse." Emma smiled at the expression on Tina's face. She loved shocking her jaded friend.

"Cute. Very cute. Even if I accept, what happens next?" Tina sounded honestly confused.

Emma was amazed, but she didn't dare show her amazement. This could actually work. "See what he suggests for the next date. If you like the idea, you say yes, and if he has no imagination and it gets boring, you say no."

She raised her hand to stop Tina when she saw her open her mouth to argue. "It's not a commitment. It's just dinner. Plenty of people have men stay over after sex, and it doesn't mean any more than the guy was too tired or too drunk to drive home. What's the big deal?

"So he saw your stuff and brushed his teeth in your bathroom. It's not saying *I do*. Believe me, *I do* takes a lot more work than a session of tooth brushing." Emma sat back in her chair at just the thought of how hard it had been to pull the wedding plans together. And how close she'd been to allowing her fear to come between her and what she wanted. Just as Tina was doing.

Tina rubbed her fingers together. "I guess. I might be blowing this all out of proportion. I don't know what it is about this guy that gets me out of sorts. It's not like I think he wants anything more than a sexual relationship," she mused.

In a confiding manner, Emma told her, "How many times have you assured me that men don't make sex emotional? It's recreational and therapeutic, but no big deal."

"That sounds like me. And it worked for you."

"Once." *And only because he was the right guy.* But Emma wasn't going to say it aloud because she suspected Tina had finally found the right guy and couldn't admit it, especially to herself.

"And you got Tony," Tina said with satisfaction. "Even if I can't imagine why you insist on keeping him."

"I believe I'm quoting you when I say that a woman should unashamedly pursue and acquire exactly what she wants, and I wanted Tony. All you want is a good time. And that's probably all Tyler wants, too." She crossed her fingers; after all, it was only fair since Tina had gotten away with bringing The Bandit to her party by crossing her fingers.

Tina sat up. "Yes, that sounds like me. How could I forget? This is no different than any other relationship. I just have sex until I'm done with him. Nothing more. Nothing to worry about." She tapped the base of her empty glass. "That's how it's supposed to be."

"Yes."

"He's just a passing thing." Tina jiggled her leg under the table. "Someone to provide a little sexual healing, just when I thought I'd have to give in and get something from my doctor to give me a pick-me-up."

Running her fingers over the base of the wineglass, she confided, "Ever since the cruise, I just couldn't seem to get my social life back in order, until the other night."

"Social life?" Emma questioned saucily. This was good. Tina never had a dry spell when it came to men unless it had to do with an important and time-consuming case.

Pausing, Tina grinned ruefully, "Okay, so I mean sex life."

"So he fixed what ailed you, and now you want to cut him loose? Bad idea. You might need more of what he's got."

"I was just bored."

"And if you keep being bored? Why not let him entertain you for a while?"

"What if he gets attached?"

"Tyler? The man who makes women hot just walking in the door? Why would a man as sophisticated as Tyler allow his heart to get involved? How many ways are we going to go over this brief? This is Tyler the player we're talking about."

Tina nodded. "You're right. I'm thinking too much. The guy could have anyone, and according to the grapevine, he has them often."

"Then you have nothing to worry about." Emma

leaned back and then picked up her wineglass with satisfaction. When Tina figured out what hit her, she'd be good and snared, and that suited Emma just fine. Soon she expected to be standing up at an altar waiting for her best friend.

Tina discarded her glass and reached for another filled one. "I'm not worried. Any apprehension about Tyler you think you saw in me you should forget. I just lost my compass for a moment." She pointed her glass in Emma's direction "Just like you did at the rehearsal. But that was just a brief step out of character."

"Speaking of stepping out of character, how is it going at the shelter?"

"It's going okay. I've got a new client, and I know there's going to be some fireworks. A protective order just doesn't do it for these guys."

"What are you going to do?"

"We might have to get Mick back to do some security work. I feel twitchy about this one."

"What happened?"

"The husband broke three of her ribs and the boy's arm when the little guy tried to intervene. It's ugly. The guy regularly exercises in bar fights and then takes himself home to punch on his wife."

"You'll get her out of there and put him away for a while."

"I can't help her unless she makes up her mind to be helped. That's the thing."

"No one understands better than you."

Tina took a large sip of the wine. "That's the

trouble. I don't understand. Even as a child, I was nobody's doormat or punching bag."

"You were strong. And now you're being strong for these women."

Tina sighed. "I'm no hero. You're looking through those rose-colored glasses again. Every lawyer does some kind of pro-bono work. I just know this stuff. Sometimes, it's like going home. Isn't that sad?"

Emma put a hand on her friend's arm. "You're wonderful."

Just then, there was a shout from Tony and his crew. They came out in a cluster. "There's my girl," Tony said, coming to Emma's side and kissing her cheek. The other men wandered away, and Tony settled in a chair next to Emma.

"I've got to go," Tina said.

"I love you." Emma squeezed Tina's hand. "Thank you for what you did today."

Tina looked uncomfortable. "You just had a little anxiety. You've been going 24/7: you've got school so you can be my paralegal, you've been planning the wedding and you've been working part-time at the law firm. It's perfectly normal to bug out a little. You don't have to get all sappy and embarrass me."

"What? I talk about love, and you complain. I talk about sex, and you complain. Next time we'll talk about work."

"We did that, too. Remember?"

"I want to talk about sex," Tony interrupted.

"I'm outta here. You two talk about sex."

Emma watched her walk away.

Tony grabbed Emma's hand and it felt so wonderful it made her eyes tear up. If only Tina could understand. But after what she'd said tonight, it was possible that sometime soon Tina would also be someone's girl.

Unless she managed to scare Tyler off. But Emma hoped not, because she sensed this time Tina would have to dig deeply into that phenomenal strength of hers to get over him. This time, Tina the wily lawyer had outsmarted even herself, as she had no idea she had fallen for him.

4

THE RINGER on her cell phone, programmed with a sappy, romantic ring tone just for Emma, interrupted Tina's hazy dreams. She grabbed the phone reflexively and felt a sense of panic as she noted the time. "Emma? What the hell's wrong?"

"I can't sleep. I'm getting married." Emma sounded weepy. "Can you believe that I'm lucky enough to be getting married, and I owe it all to you?"

"It's 5:00 a.m. You're not getting married for twelve hours. And it's going to be an even longer day if you don't get any sleep."

"Are you kidding? I'm going to float through this day. I'll fly. It's the day I'm getting married," she repeated, wonder in her voice.

"So why didn't you call me just after midnight? That still qualified as the day you were getting married, and I was still awake then," Tina complained, settling back against her pillow.

"I'm sorry. I'm just so excited I thought I might burst if I didn't share it with my best friend."

Tina winced. She'd never meant to have a best

friend; it had just sort of happened. And she didn't like getting in so deep. She didn't quite know what do with relationships. What if she let Emma down? "Why don't you call the groom?"

"I can't. I'm not going to see or hear from him today, not until the wedding tonight."

Tina yawned. "Ah, that superstitious crap." And then realizing she was treading on Emma's superstitious crap, she backtracked. "Do you need me to do anything for you today? Anything last minute?"

"No, I just wanted to hear your voice. You're the sister of my heart, and I wanted to share this terrifying moment with you."

"You're still feeling scared?" Tina sat up, thinking she was the one who should be scared considering she didn't even know what the sister of a heart was.

"I'm scared to death." But Emma didn't sound scared. "I'm also thrilled to death. It's all rolled up in a package inside of me. Have you ever felt that way?"

"I guess. Before I took the bar exam."

Emma laughed. "It doesn't even begin to compare. Are you sure you won't come to the spa today and have the complete treatment before the wedding?"

Tina shuddered at the thought. "I'm not a masochist."

"You like to look nice. I know you'd like the massage and the manicure. I've even got an appointment with Henry to have my hair done."

"I can take the spa treatment. What I can't take is all the girly talk." She yawned. "Though I think I could stand it if it was just you."

Emma laughed. "Why, thank you. If you change your mind, you know where I'll be."

"I'm not going to go to the spa with a bunch of giddy women before a wedding. Absolutely not." *Even if you say sentimental things that touch my heart.*

"Well, then, go back to sleep, girlfriend, and I'll see you soon."

"Go back to sleep?" Tina groused. "Just go back to sleep and have sweet dreams. How can you be so cruel?"

Emma just laughed again as if Tina had said something warm and fuzzy and hadn't just turned her down and then complained.

Tina hung up the phone. Of course, she couldn't sleep. She tossed and turned until she'd tied her six-hundred-count ecru Egyptian sheets into knots.

After two cups of espresso, she felt charged and ready, but had nothing to do since she'd cleared Emma's wedding day on her calendar, only to find out about the spa thing too late. The digital clock seemed to be standing still, and her mind was jumping with philosophical crap.

Should a person risk commitment? Of course, there was no answer. Each person had to make up their own mind and take their own chances. She could never take such a chance. Every marriage she'd seen during her days as a foster child had seemed dismal at best.

Thoughts of commitment somehow brought Tyler to mind and by 7:00 a.m. she was going crazy, so she called him. After all, misery loved company. "Hey, Tyler, are you sleeping?"

"Not anymore, unfortunately." His voice always sounded kinda gravelly when he'd just woken up.

"Have you got a leggy blonde wrapped around you or are you alone?"

"Do you really care?"

"No. I'm just trying to be sensitive. Emma says I have to work on that part of my personality."

"I can't imagine why."

"Anyway, if you're free, I though we might go for a run on the beach before it gets hot."

"What?"

"A run. The beach. Didn't you tell me on the cruise that you like to run on the beach some mornings?"

"I'm flattered you remember anything about the cruise since you rarely refer to it. Yes. I run on the beach, and yes, I'd like to run on the beach this morning."

"Oh." She hadn't actually thought he'd go for it. "Okay. Do you want to start at the bait shop you mentioned? We can get one last shot of caffeine before you eat my sand."

"Is this going to be a competitive sport?"

"I don't know. Are you feeling competitive?"

"Honey, you always bring out the best in me. I'll meet you in an hour."

She hung up the phone thinking there was actually a smile in his voice. At seven o'clock on a Saturday morning. When she'd woken him up for no good reason. Obviously, the man was a nutcase. But at this point, she'd do anything to pass the time and keep from thinking too much.

AT THE BAIT SHOP, Tyler wondered what Tina wore to run in. He wouldn't admit it to her—as it made him a dog—but he could imagine she'd come in spandex that clung to her sleek figure. He couldn't seem to get enough of her. Even though she was probably through with him.

So it was strange, but exhilarating, that she'd called him. She'd even mentioned the cruise, which she usually refused to acknowledged. Tina was a tough sell. But he intended to pursue her. The pup at his feet was weapon number one. Tyler leaned down to pet both his dogs.

The beach was as fine as his mood. The sun felt warm shining down on him. Neither the heat nor the humidity had really kicked in this morning. The waves rolled in, and though the sound of the water usually relaxed him, he found himself shifting from runner to runner waiting impatiently for her little red BMW to swing into the lot.

He was gone on her. Just seeing that jaunty car in the parking lot at the courthouse or the district attorney's office gave him a lift.

"There she is, boys," he said as the little car pulled up. "Don't let me down. I'm counting on you to help me win the lady."

Tina brought the car to a stop practically at his feet. Then she just sat there as the engine died. The top of the little car was down and he felt like a voyeur when she ran her fingers through her tousled hair. Then she licked those lush lips and he felt like going down on his knees and begging. He wanted those fingers running over his body. He wanted to drink the coffee she'd mentioned from those lips. He wanted. It had become a litany. When had he become so pathetic?

"You're early." She got out of the car sounding as if she hadn't noticed her effect on him.

She wasn't wearing spandex but the little shorts and top looked hot.

"For some reason, I was wide awake at 7:00 a.m."

"I'm supposed to be doing female bonding before the wedding, but I couldn't take it." She fidgeted.

He'd never seen her fidget. Was it possible that she needed more than a morning run? Weddings had a tendency to ignite the romantic imaginings of women. And for women, romance led to sex. Tina might not be the romantic type, but she still might be feeling the thrill.

"Exercise is good for stress." He tried to act as if he wasn't turned on by the thought of fulfilling any of Tina's romantic or sexual needs.

However, when Tina made eye contact with a familiar, intent look in her eyes, he got even more excited. Was she really considering letting off a little sexual steam? Was that why she'd called him?

He held his breath as she turned to look over at him and then lowered her sunglasses to examine the boys panting at his feet. Would she appreciate his surprise?

Weren't puppies considered romantic?

But she held up her hands in apparent denial. "No, way, Tyler. No way am I going running with you and those animals. I don't do dogs."

Her dismissive tone made him realize he'd read her

wrong on every level. It seemed the upcoming wedding made Tina feel combative. This woman was spoiling for a fight. Not romance.

Well, he enjoyed a challenge, and right now he'd take her any way he could get her. He loved how her company stimulated him. Tina's flair for the dramatic made other women seem boring.

Tyler smiled widely, knowing it would immediately get a rise out of her. "These are not just any dogs. They're purebred Labs. Roy is the older, black Lab and Frosty's our new addition. He's a white Lab and still young enough to be a little excitable."

She took off her sunglasses and pointed with them. "That one can't possibly run on the beach. It's only a pup."

"Congratulations. You do know something about dogs. Actually, he's eight weeks old, and his name is Frosty."

"You already said that," she informed him drily.

"Well, he's the one who's supposed to steal your heart, since you won't allow me to do it." Tyler picked up the squirming puppy, who instantly reached up to give him a bath with his tongue. "We can leave him in the back of the truck for a little while if you really want to run full out."

"Don't let him do that." Tina looked appalled. "He's got germs."

"Do what?"

"He's licking you. Are you crazy?"

"He does it all the time. Don't tell me you're afraid

of a little puppy slobber? You're not wimping out on me, are you? Is this the same woman who dragged me out of bed and challenged me to a run this morning?"

That ought to ignite her temper from the slow burn to an outright fight.

She pushed her hair back. "Well, I'm sorry about calling you at the crack of dawn. It was Emma's fault. She called me first. See, she had it all planned out, but I just couldn't go to the spa with a bunch of babbling women. You should see them, they gush and they hug and…" She shuddered. "I don't even know what I'm doing here. Emma's gone and made me a crazed lunatic with all of her girly talk."

"What's this about Emma? Isn't she getting married today?"

"Later. Six o'clock. Black tie. The works. It's going to be beautiful, and we didn't have to pick out the dreaded bridesmaids' dresses. There were plenty of gorgeous black formals to choose from. Plus, we aren't wearing exactly the same gown. Each is flattering to the woman, similar and yet individual."

He grinned widely. Apparently, she'd done a considerable amount of work on her sales pitch in order to convince Emma.

Tina took a step back against the car. "You're smiling. Why?"

He prevaricated. "You were gushing a little, and I was enjoying it. It was very feminine and cute."

She held her hands up. "I don't do cute."

Tyler leaned closer and let Frosty brush up against

her. "He does cute. He's about to jump out of my arms to get to you. Do you want to hold him?"

Seeming to evaluate her options she reached out a tentative hand to stroke the pup. "Frosty?"

"Yeah, he's going to stay nearly white when he's grown, and his dad had this cool attitude. But I'm afraid this pup doesn't have a shred of dignity. He's more of a lover."

"He's soft." She stroked his ears. "Especially his ears."

You're soft. "Haven't you ever had a puppy?"

Her eyes went all golden as she petted the pup. He wished she'd look in his direction with those wide vulnerable eyes. *He'd be happy to pet her.*

"No. Not that belonged to me."

"A hamster, a gerbil, a goldfish or a bird? Nothing?"

She shook her head and took her hand away, but Frosty whined and struggled against Tyler's chest so she tentatively resumed rubbing his ears. "You're right, he's shameless."

I'll be shameless.

Frosty lunged, and Tyler sort of let him go. Tina reached out and caught him in her arms before he fell to the ground.

"You have to hold on tighter," she scolded as she hoisted the fat puppy high in her arms.

"You can hold on."

She looked adorably flustered, as if she could read his thoughts.

"I thought we were going to run."

Tyler nodded and then went around to the back of

his truck. "Okay, put him in the kennel, and we'll go." He reached down to pet Roy where he'd secured him to the tow bar. "Roy can still keep up."

"But it'll get too hot for him in the kennel."

"Not really, not yet, anyway. Just stick him in the kennel."

She struggled to put the wriggling pup in the kennel and then closed it with a little flourish. She pushed her hair back again. "Do you go through that every time?"

"Just until he gets used to it." He closed the hatch.

As if on cue the pup immediately began a long sad howl, ending in little yips.

"Why's he doing that?"

"He's lonely. He'll be fine." Tyler untied Roy. "This is Roy. He's friendly, and he doesn't give you a bath. At least not until he shakes water all over you."

Tina absently petted Roy but she kept looking back at the truck where Frosty was crying mournfully.

"I want to run, but what if he gets stolen? It's not like he's being discreet back there."

Tyler shrugged.

As if Frosty could sense they were discussing him, his howls rose in crescendo.

"Okay, I'm a sucker, but you have to let him out of there. He's disturbing the peace or something," Tina muttered.

Tyler hid his smile as he took the pup out of the kennel. Of course, he never had any intention of leaving the pup behind. He was being unabashedly sneaky, but with Tina he needed every advantage.

Holding the puppy up, he told her, "See, he stopped howling the minute I put my fingers on the latch."

"He's okay?"

"He's manipulating us." And Tyler didn't feel remotely guilty for attempting to manipulate Tina.

"Now what do we do with him? Does he come with a leash?"

"You carry him along the beach while he does some sight-seeing. I'm afraid it means walking, not running."

"You carry him. The pets really do own the masters. Maybe that's why I never had one. I don't intend to be owned by anyone. Ever."

It sounded like fair warning, but Tyler never backed down from a challenge. "You can practice, just for the day."

"Just for today," she parroted, as she settled the pup against her hip.

He followed along in her wake, holding Roy's leash, and thank his lucky stars for whatever had caused her companionable mood. "So you chose me over some wedding thing?"

"A morning at the spa where they admire each other's manicures, talk about the shape of each other's cuticles, and discuss dreams of marriage and picket fences." She rolled her eyes. "Women expect marriage to fulfill them, even when they appear happy in their career. It always floors me."

He nudged her shoulder. "You're right. If someone's lonely, they should just get themselves a puppy."

Tina lifted Frosty like an offering. "Right. He's

turning out to be great company: so far he's washed off all of my sunscreen and scratched my arms."

"I could reapply your sunscreen. Diligently."

"I'll bet. You foisted him off on me on purpose. I never fell for that ploy of putting him in the kennel. You wouldn't have done that."

"Guilty as charged. But you're a hard woman and I needed reinforcements this morning to show you what a nice guy I am."

"Reinforcement. That's what I forgot. Coffee. You should be glad I had a hit before I left the house. I'm a dragon without my coffee."

"I'll buy you whatever type of caffeine you need when we get back to the bait shop."

She shifted Frosty to the other hip. "He's surprisingly heavy. What'll he do if I put him down on the sand?"

"Run a bit, dig a bit, nibble on things. Puppy stuff."

Putting Frosty down on the sand, she stepped back as if he might explode, jump up, or do something interesting. Instead he whined a bit and plopped down. Not moving.

Tina looked at the dog. He was cute, but he didn't do much. Why would anyone want one of these things? She remembered with no fondness picking up crap in the backyard of more than one foster home with a dog—most of them mean dogs. At least this one was cute. Nudging Frosty with her foot, she said, "Come on, dog. I've got to walk at least, or I won't be able to pig out on wedding cake, and it's Italian cream cake."

She could feel Tyler breathing down her neck,

watching to see if his machinations were working. The man was actively sneaky. She should never have admitted any admiration for his stripper routine. It seemed to have gone to his head. "Why isn't he moving?"

"I think he liked being in your arms. I know I like it."

Now there was a thought. It was nice in Tyler's arms, too. "Humph, well, if I carry him, then it counts as something. Not aerobic, but I'll think of it as weight training."

"You don't need to train. You're beautiful just as you are."

The nice little tingle became more intense. It was amazing how she responded to this man—even when she didn't recognize him, as she hadn't the other night. It must be what they referred to as chemistry. And of course, chemistry was a short-lived phenomenon. But while it lasted, maybe he could help her with this little itch she'd acquired as a side effect to all of the romance she'd been exposed to last night. Even Emma would approve.

As if he could read her mind, or maybe her body language, he stroked the back of her neck, just where she liked it.

The man certainly paid attention. Leaning into his touch, she thought he might be good to have for brunch, but she didn't want him to know what she had in mind, not just yet. "Back off, counselor, unless you want me to sue you for sexual harassment."

"It would be worth it."

"I said *run* not *fun* on the beach." She bent down.

Tyler's smile contained a certain amount of heat. She figured he'd gotten a charge from viewing her cleavage as she'd squatted to scoop up Frosty. Good for him, and eventually, good for her, too. "Down boy."

"Can I help it that it's such a beautiful…day?"

"Don't men ever think about anything else?" She held up the pup and looked at Tyler challengingly. How hard was he willing to work for it? It was going to be tough to top The Bandit encounter. In fact, why had she worried about seeing him? He could never bring her to that level again. It had been all about the fantasy. Nothing more.

"Not really."

Grinning at his honesty as she stroked the pup's incredibly soft fur, she remembered how Tyler had used faux fur on her skin. She'd thought she would die from the pleasure of the silly stuff.

"Your eyes go all golden when you're aroused. It's the biggest turn-on."

"I guess I could let you turn me on."

He moved in closer, and she pulled the puppy higher as a shield. "Let's walk for a while."

"Will you talk with me?"

Gripping the pup tightly enough to make him grunt, she asked, "What do you want to talk about?"

"The wedding? Is that an okay topic for this morning?"

"I guess. Just don't go getting sentimental on me. Please? I don't know what it is about milestones that make perfectly regular people act all gooey."

"I absolutely, unequivocally, positively promise not to be gooey."

They walked. And the conversation flowed more

easily than she would have thought. She told him about Emma's bout of anxiety at the wedding rehearsal. How she thought she might not be able to give Tony children, and how Tony's easy acceptance had defused the situation. "So I had to walk down the aisle with the matchstick cousin. It's hard to tell if he's in a state of perpetual blush, or if it's the acne. Poor kid. He seems nice enough."

"And Tony?" Tyler asked.

"I guess Tony is a good guy." She sighed. "He's not good enough for Emma, but at least I'm not disappointed. I know she'll probably get her heart broken down the line, because she's the loyal type, and she believes in forever. But at least he's a good guy going in."

"Wow. Your confidence in your fellow man is amazing."

"My confidence in my fellow man *is* amazing. It just doesn't extend to marriage. I've seen the inside of quite a few and I think it's a farce that hurts a lot more people than it helps."

"And is there any room in your personal philosophy for love?" He reached over and stroked the puppy.

The fact that her breast happened to be swelling beneath the puppy and that his fingers wandered over Frosty to stroke her nipple was obviously no accident.

She stood as still as possible, enjoying his touch. "There's no such thing as love, just varying degrees of lust."

"Are you feeling lust now?" He rolled her nipple

between his finger and thumb in the shelter of the puppy's body.

"Oh, yeah," she breathed.

He leaned down and bit her gently and seductively on the neck. "You taste so good. Sweet and salty."

Alarmed at the way her knees went weak when his breath feathered over her skin, she looked around them. Fortunately, they had the beach mostly to themselves.

He moved closer. "If I take you home and ply you with caffeine, can I have my wicked way with you?"

She ran her hand up his thigh to stroke his penis through his shorts. He immediately sprang to attention. "I'm not sure I want to wait," she whispered.

Just then two little girls came stampeding down the beach in their general direction. Tina removed her hand and took a step back from him.

Focusing on the sand-covered little girls, Tyler looked just like a doting uncle. "You like kids?" Tina laughed.

"What's not to like?"

Tina looked at the disheveled children, the youngest with a sodden diaper hanging between her legs. "You're kidding, right? Don't make eye contact, and maybe they'll disappear as quickly as they showed up."

"Don't you like kids?"

"Actually, I do like kids. I just doubt a hotshot lawyer man like you would."

"The hotshot lawyer woman is sexist. And the kids are headed in this direction. Odds are that they've spotted the puppy."

Tina looked up to see a very pregnant mother

waddling toward them. "Maybe their mother will take them away."

"Poor thing. She'll just be glad of the distraction for a little while."

TYLER HATED TO SEE the little girls go, afraid they'd take this softer version of Tina with them. She'd spent at least twenty minutes frolicking on the beach with the girls while their worn-out mother sat on the sand. He mused that Tina had more fun than the young ones, including Frosty. She even looked like a little girl, with her hair flat on one side and a smudge of sand on her cheek. However, her laughter hit him in visceral places as the kids threw themselves on her.

Finally, Frosty plopped down exhausted, and the girls ran away, laughing, with their mother in tow.

Tyler came over and sat down, skin to skin with Tina. She pushed him away. "You're all sandy."

"*I'm* all sandy?"

She grinned. "Okay, so I'm a little messy. Boy, those girls really loved Frosty."

Frosty wagged his tale at the sound of his name and struggled up to come and snuggle beside her leg.

"All little kids love puppies. It's that instinctive thing. But they loved you more."

"Right." She shrugged it off. "We all know how it works. Puppies and babies have pheromones meant to make the average sap totally gullible. Otherwise, we would pitch them into the nearest trash can the first time they pooped all over themselves."

He choked out a laugh. "That's pretty harsh, darlin'." He watched as she rubbed at her face. "Don't you want children?"

"Eventually."

Reaching down, he brushed the sand off her cheek. "I know you're not as tough as you pretend."

Glaring at him, she picked up a handful of sand. "Don't kid yourself. I'll use this."

"I dare you."

She launched herself at him with her hand cocked and ready to release the sand in his direction, only she'd forgotten the pup, and she tripped trying not to squash him. Coming up out of the sand even more bedraggled than before, she whined, "Look at me. I'm covered in sand and salt."

"You're a mess." But he didn't fall for her whining. He figured she'd fling sand just as soon as he showed her sympathy. Tina thought she played fair, but with her face and figure she was lethal, and it was anything but fair. In fact, he wanted nothing more than to roll around in the sand with her.

"It's your fault," she accused. "You had the bright idea of bringing that maniac dog to the beach."

"I just thought we'd go for a walk, not wallow in the sand."

She dug her hand into the wet sand until she had a huge handful, and then she slung it at him. He tried to get out of the way but it hit him on the shoulder, and sand and water ran down his T-shirt.

"There, now you're a mess, too."

He scooped up his own handful of sand but she got up and ran into the surf screaming. He followed her in until they were both knee deep, and then he rubbed the sand on the back of her arm.

"Yuck! I've got a wedding in a few hours and you rub sand on my arm."

"Just think it's exfoliating your skin with every grain. I've just saved you a fortune at that spa, plus putting up with all of that girly relationship talk."

She turned to look at him. "All those girls want is a big, strong hero like you to come along and save them. What idiots. Heroes only complicate things."

"I don't know. I could be your hero."

"What makes you think I need a hero? Do you know what a girl who doesn't believe in heroes does?"

"What?" Would she finally open up and tell him something about her past?

"She learns to fight for herself." She threw a huge handful of seaweed that caught him across the face. "Got you!"

Then she took off running.

"Not fair." He felt around for his own seaweed and found a big gooey clump with the yellow pods. "But I'm going to get *you*."

Tina screeched, sounding a lot like those little girls. She also got a lead on him.

"Hey, wait up. If we get too deep Frosty might run away or try to catch us," he shouted.

Immediately she turned toward shore, running in the surf with her clothes clinging to her. He followed closely in her wake. And when she was looking for Frosty, Tyler came up behind her and stuffed a big, gross, handful of seaweed down inside of her collar.

"Ooooh, don't. I'm looking out for the dumb dog."

"He's over beside Roy." The exhausted dogs were actually watching them as if they were confused by the wild antics of the humans.

"Then it won't hurt if I do this." Tina put a glop of wet sand down his pants.

"And I'm going to do the same." He grabbed her as she tried to run away. "I'm going to rub the sand on your pretty little ass until you beg me to stop."

She went totally still. "And why would I do a stupid thing like beg you to stop?"

He stood like a statue with the forgotten sand dribbling through his fingers.

Sidling up to him, she rubbed up against him, much like Frosty would have but with totally different results. "Don't," he protested softly. "Those little girls."

"They're long gone. No one is close by."

"It's not a good idea." Though his body thought it was the only idea. He couldn't seem to catch his breath.

"Why not? I like having your hands on me." She took his sandy fingers and rubbed them against the smooth skin of her abdomen. Then she stepped deeper into the surf. "But we better get a little deeper."

He followed, as obedient as Roy. Even though he knew he might flounder.

When they were up to their chests in the water Tina took his hand and then put it up under her sports bra.

The nipple puckered under his sand-roughened fingers, and she leaned into him, almost humming with tension.

He didn't hesitate to slide his other hand up under the sodden material and caress the cool flesh. Then he reached down and kissed her until he tasted woman seasoned by salt.

"Ummmm," she moaned, her hands sliding around his back, coming to rest on his butt, and then giving it a squeeze. "You *do* have a way with your hands."

He slid the sports bra back in place, then slid his hands lower and slipped them around until she was fully against him. Every curve fitted deliciously against his aroused body, and she obligingly rested up against him.

"And a way with your cock." She rubbed his penis through the shorts he had on until it strained against the material.

"It's a gift," he panted in her ear, wishing she didn't affect him so much that his brain refused to engage. Being with her was dangerous, but he wanted it. Wanted every challenge she represented.

"And I'm going to prove it to you." He pushed her backward until the water lapped the tops of her collarbones. Then he put his hands on the edge of her bra, easing it up over the mounds of her breasts to caresses her erect nipples until her breathing was erratic, and his body was screaming for release.

Then he kissed her, a kiss slow and deep and hungry. "I want you so badly." He picked her up just as a swell threatened to splash her face.

"There's no one on the beach who's paying attention." Those golden eyes looked at him so intently. So trustingly?

He shuddered with pleasure at the thought of entering the heat of her body while surrounded by the cool, restless surf.

"Let's go closer to shore."

"Why?" He could hardly think for the desire swamping him.

"I want to straddle you in the surf. I want you deep inside of me." She pushed him toward the shore.

"I may just drown, but I'll die happy." Her desire made him feel incredibly powerful, even as he willingly followed along.

As they approached the shore, he pulled her to a stop and then dragged her down on top of him. The knee-high surf boiled up around them as he touched her all over, as she ground the heat of her body against him. It took a few awkward seconds for him to release his penis from the clinging shorts, and then he pressed it against her. "Oh, you feel so good," he groaned.

"Tyler." On her knees in front of him, she grabbed his shaft under the water and squeezed gently and then more firmly.

He might go off, he thought, just explode like the water around them.

"This is pretty bold of us," she told him, looking into his eyes, squeezing his cock with her hands. She glanced out at the beach. "Do you have adventurous sex all the time? I'm not sure I can keep up."

"Tina." It was a plea. He was barely hanging on and only because he wanted her with him when he came.

She stood up, the sports bra in place though her nipples were like pebbles through the material. "Do you want me to take off my shorts?" It was a whisper within the roar of the water, but she might have screamed it.

"Please." He tasted salt, and he wished he were someplace where he could taste her, sate himself with her essence. Lying open to him on the beach, she would taste tantalizing.

"Did you bring protection?"

He shook his head. "No. Damn! I didn't think you'd—we'd—do this on the beach."

She pulled a condom out of the back pocket of her shorts and handed it to him.

"You just happened to bring a condom?"

She shook her head. "I bought it out of the restroom machine while the girls played with Frosty. I couldn't help it. I really want you."

It was dicey. Salt and sand made the condom stick and balk. Then there were the waves, and a possible audience from the beach. However, Tina shielded his body with hers, and her hands rubbed hungrily on his skin, offering a huge incentive.

"Okay." He lowered himself into the water. "We're good to go."

"My turn. I'm gonna take off these shorts."

He turned to look at the beach but didn't see anyone close enough to see what they were doing.

Ducking down into the water, Tina moved this

way and then that way, until she held the shorts up out of the water.

"Success."

"Come here. Before I die from wanting you."

"Okay, but I'm in charge." When she obviously thought he was going to argue, she hurried on to say, "Darlin' I'm going to ride you like you're a horse. Is that what you have in mind? Does that work for you?"

"I don't have a mind." His body thrummed. He couldn't think.

She drifted down and toward him. He guided her, running worshiping hands down over her cloth-covered nipples, then the smooth skin of her abdomen, and then between her legs to her heat. She was burning hot, and the water was cool around his chest. Spray teased his mouth as he looked at her face.

"Don't," she breathed as he put pressure on her clit where he knew she craved it.

"Why?" he gasped.

"We can't take too long, and I want your cock so badly I can't think."

She did. He could feel the thick moisture of her body as he stroked her under the water. "You want me now?"

"Yes." She positioned herself over his legs so that his cock rubbed against her.

"Right now?"

"Yes." She gave a sexy little moan as she slid onto the length of his penis.

He leaned forward to kiss her mouth and she pulled slightly away.

"If you do that anyone who goes by us will figure out what we're doing."

"Do I care?" He pulled on her hips, bringing her flush with his body. "Is that too deep?" There were other ways to possess her.

"No, oh." She clung to him.

Clutching the firm curve of her ass he brought them together, deeper and harder. "Is this what you want?"

"It's so good. The pressure of the water and the full length of you. Oh, Tyler. Please."

He leaned close and licked the salt off her ear. Pulling and then pushing, until she had his rhythm. It wasn't much different than the surf going back and forth around them. Only more insistent.

She pulled his hair and arched closer. He bit his lip and tightened his grip. Their urgent noises were swallowed by the surf, and despite her fear, he kissed her at their climax, taking her scream into his mouth and her surrender into his heart.

A few moments later she lifted her head from his shoulder, and he felt a strong sense of loss. "Well, Tyler, you *are* full of surprises."

At that moment, a large wave smacked them, sending them tumbling into the surf.

When the world stopped swirling, he got his legs and shorts in place, laughing, giddy. "Are you okay?"

She lifted her arms in the air, free of her usual restraint. "I'm great." Then she grinned like a naughty little girl. "Only I seemed to have lost my shorts in the foam."

"Really?" He looked around, wondering what they were going to do without her clothing.

"There!" She pointed, and he waded out to retrieve them. When he got back to her she laughed and threw her arms around his neck. "My hero," she proclaimed.

He felt another wave of desire as she hung from him, warm skin plastered to him. Would it always be this intense with her? He thought it would because *she* was intense. Dramatic. He'd never again be bored because she had a kind of coiled energy that charged him. "I want you again," he whispered.

"I think we've already pushed our luck to the limit."

"Can I see you later?"

"I've got a wedding, remember?"

"Why didn't you put me on the guest list? I had to crash the shower."

"Yeah, you came as the office bimbo's date. Don't remind me or I'm liable to smack you."

"Right now, I can't remember anyone other than you." He ran his hand over her ass and between her cheeks, seeking her heat.

She pulled away. "No. Down, boy."

"I'm sorry. I'm not usually such a dog."

Bending down and sliding into her shorts under the water, she shot him a look. "I don't mind it when you're a dog. In fact, I like what you do to me. And I'm very fond of your willingness to improvise."

He brought a finger to his chin. "There's an elevator in my office building I could imagine us putting to good use."

"Anything else?"

He rubbed his hands together. "I'll make a list."

"And I'll enjoy checking it twice."

A large wave rocked her. "Whoa, the tide is definitely coming in," Tina said with a teasing light in those luminous eyes. "I'm glad it waited for us to finish."

"So the underwater adventure was to the lady's satisfaction."

"I had an orgasm, if that's what you mean. I didn't think you could come close to The Bandit thing, but you did." She waded out of the water and then bent down to pet the puppy.

She'd doubted he could repeat The Bandit thing? She didn't know him very well. "It would save time and energy showering together. I'll even rub you down with exfoliant from an actual bottle. You can tell Emma that you had your own personal spa slave to help you get ready for the nuptials."

She didn't look up. "I'd like to, but I can't."

In fact she suddenly seemed deflated.

He sat down beside her and the puppy. Roy came up wagging his tail. "You don't seem excited about the wedding."

"Wishes and magic. That's what she wants."

"That's what most people want when they get married."

"Why? Does it help them through the arguments and disappointments later on?"

"I think so."

"I didn't make it easier. I couldn't give her everything she wanted when she reached out to me."

There was a lost expression on her face when she lifted her head from where she knelt in the sand.

"What is it, baby?" Tina vulnerable was more potent than he'd ever imagined, and he suddenly felt frightened by the depth of feeling building up inside him like the base of a giant wave. Falling for Tina would be exactly like crashing on the sand.

She didn't seem to notice his reaction. Instead, tears spilled from her lashes. "I'm not crying. It's just the salt water bothering my eyes." She rubbed her eyes until they cleared.

"Of course. The salt."

Those eyes clouded up again. "She called me the sister of her heart. What the hell am I supposed to do with that?"

"What do you think you have to do?"

"I could tell she wanted me to answer her. Reciprocate or something." She pushed her wet hair back from her face. "She called me on the eve of her wedding to say she loved me. Instead of telling her something sentimental, I folded."

Lowering her head, she muttered, "I suck as a friend."

Frosty wriggled his way into her lap, and then he licked her face until she was forced to look up.

Without fanfare, Tina leaned her head against Tyler's shoulder, and the world changed for him, forever.

Just like that.

Crash and burn or not.

"What do you think you should have said?" He hoped she didn't notice how his voice trembled.

"That I loved her or something?"

Her voice was cutting, but he didn't care because her hair lay over his shoulder like a soft shawl, and he could feel her breath against his heart.

A heart that had somehow come to belong to her.

"I don't think Emma needs you to say anything. That's the kind of friendship you have."

"But shouldn't I be able to give her something back?"

"Don't you already?"

She pulled away to look at him. "The words. The words are important to some people."

"How long have you been friends with Emma?"

"I don't know. I don't like to have friends. They take work and time, but she kinda snuck up on me. We had a few conversations, lunch, and then wham, you know, she had my phone number, she called to say hello, and next thing I know, I had a friend. And I couldn't say no, because saying no to Emma would be like kicking Frosty." Tina rubbed the puppy's ears until he whimpered in ecstasy.

"This is actually her fault," Tina complained. "I warned her that I don't do the friend thing."

"Then it's definitely her fault. How long?"

"A few years, I guess."

"Then I would say Emma knows exactly what she's going to get from you, and it's not pretty words."

She turned to him again. His heart contracted in his chest. "Really?"

He tugged on her hair. "Unless you've changed significantly in the past few years."

Tina shook her head. "If I've changed at all, it's her fault. She's been trying to turn me into a sap. Just ask her about the stupid cry movie she made me watch, and it's her fault I danced with you on the ship. I have strict rules about lawyers…."

He pulled her chin up, and then kissed her lips very, very gently. "Remind me to give her my eternal thanks."

She pulled away just a little bit. "Don't go soft and mushy on me, or I'll regret I ever called you up. If I wanted mush, I'd have gone to the spa with the women."

Pressing his lips together to avoid bursting out laughing, he looked over her tousled head as she lounged with the puppy on the sand. She was tough all right, but with a soft center.

This answered every one of his questions about Tina. Not only did she have a soft side, it was just as enticing as her beautiful body. She challenged his mind and engaged his heart. Now, if only he could convince her to open up to him. Then he wouldn't have to worry about crashing. He could ride the wave forever.

But how to get to a woman with an incredibly tough shell?

"Tina, about that lobster dinner? Have you reconsidered?"

She looked up and then tilted her head to one side, assessing him. "I guess so, since you really do owe me. But you'll have to schedule it with my assistant. I'm pretty booked up this week and next."

He nodded, pleased. One fancy dinner with foreplay as an appetizer should make her melt for him. He'd pleasure her physically until she couldn't think, and then he'd keep her warm and fuzzy until she realized that he'd found his way into her heart.

He'd be patient and impossible to refuse, just like Emma. And one day, Tina would look at him with that vulnerable, confused look on her face, as she moved her stuff into his house.

Or he moved in with her.

Or he'd simply take her things one item at a time until she just got tired of fighting him and missed her clothes and her bed.

Tina might be tough, but he was very, very persistent.

5

TINA FELT the interlude on the beach had cleared her mind and taken the ache from her heart. Yes, she almost felt misty as she walked down the aisle on the arm of the thirteen-year-old whose pimples seemed to have reached the Vesuvius level and whose jerky stride kept pulling her off her mountainous heels.

Thank goodness for the kid. He was keeping her emotionally, if not physically, stable.

She grinned.

That smile disappeared the moment they got to the stairs leading to the altar. That's where he stepped on the edge of her gown and tripped her. Fortunately, he was stronger than he looked and caught her by the arm before she hit the ground. He held her up while she caught her breath. A minute later they were calm and composed and ready for the bride, as if there had been no glitch in their stride.

"She looks so beautiful," Tina whispered as Emma came down the aisle on her father's arm, a sight to see as she'd had a tenuous relationship with the man since her parents' divorce.

Slowly, Emma came forward with a look on her face that held all of her hopes and dreams for the future. Glowing, she reached out for her groom as if she was positive he had all the answers of her heart and would always treasure them.

Tina felt the cracks in her armor widen as she watched the sister of her heart pledge her life to a man who looked at her as if she'd dropped like a star from the sky. Tina bit down hard on her lip to keep from crying. And at that moment she was grateful for the easily intimidated teenage escort, who wouldn't dare to tell if he saw a stray tear on the face of the maid of honor.

AFTER THE WEDDING, Tina danced with all the men in the wedding party including the teenager, who was actually a decent dancer and seemed to have developed a crush on her. The wedding cake was delicious, and so was watching the groom laugh out loud as Emma gave him a huge bite of cake that tumbled down the front of his tux.

Those tender looks the bride and groom exchanged tugged at Tina's heart. And she got a thrill when Emma came and whispered in her ear that she and Tony were sneaking away because they simply couldn't wait another minute to start their lives together. Emma squeezed her hand and whispered that she'd thought of such a daring thing because of Tina's influence.

It wasn't the mushy exchange Tina expected, rather just a sweet compliment and parting squeeze. Then, wide-eyed and obviously feeling cheeky, the bride snuck out of the party with one last wink.

Tina felt as if she'd somehow offered something precious to her friend. Trust Emma to give Tina a gift even on her own big day.

In fact, Tina had been feeling so mushy that after a few glasses of wine she took her phone out of her little bag and gave Tyler a call. "Hey, Tyler. Gotta date tonight?"

"No. I couldn't seem to get invited to a wedding I was interested in, so I'm having dinner with my dogs."

"How's Frosty as a companion? Which network does he like? Disney Channel?"

"He loves Scooby Doo. Why are you calling me? I thought you were doing a wedding thing."

"Emma snuck out. It was most brazen of her, but she did it. I'm so proud of her." Tina sniffed. "It's definitely the wine."

"Do you want to bring me a piece of cake?"

"That's pretty bold of you, asking for cake when I'm not even sure I'm coming over to see you."

"Please? Frosty and I are just wild about frosting."

"Cute. You are so cute. In fact, I've been thinking about how cute you look. Naked."

"And how do you look in your dress? I'll bet you're incredibly hot. Does it plunge in any interesting directions? Will I be able to help you undress with one easy pull of a zipper, or is it a modest pearl button?"

"Aren't you good at women's clothing?" She chuckled. "Well, it's no surprise to me. Will you be disappointed if it's the modest pearl button?"

"I'm spectacular with women's clothing. And modest just leaves lots to the imagination."

"It's an expensive dress. You'd have to help me out of it with the utmost care."

"Absolutely. I'd treat the fabric with great respect—even if I'm imagining ripping the dress off with my teeth."

It was a seductive suggestion.

And that suggestion gave her a little chill down her spine where there was just a little keyhole opening in the dress. He wouldn't be disappointed, and neither, she imagined, would she. "You didn't have enough of me then? In the sand and the surf?"

"Never. I'm still hungry enough to want to nibble all along your body. I only wish you were still covered with salt and foam. Please come over. I'm begging. With all this talk about your sexy black dress—and if you're wearing garters, I swear I'll get down on my knees."

"Ah, the man loves garters. Well, I just happen…" An argument suddenly caught her attention, a boisterous exchange that seemed to have gotten heated very quickly. "Sorry, Tyler. I've got to call you back. There's a fight about to break out." Then she snapped the face back into place.

With the phone cradled in her hand, she watched the exchange. Calling the police at Emma's wedding would be a shame, but Emma wasn't here to be upset, and she wouldn't enjoy any extra expense if there was damage to the very exclusive reception hall.

"You've been after him since we were in high

school." A man in a tight suit yelled at a woman in a
brown dress that made her look like an overcooked
sausage. "You're always looking at other men."

The woman yelled back in rapid Spanish.

Sighing, Tina thought, *same tune, different lyrics.*
It took her back to a small, stuffy kitchen that perpetu-
ally smelled like bacon grease no matter how long
she'd scrubbed at the chipped counters. Mr. Granger
would yell at Mrs. Granger about everything from
having an affair with the neighbor's boy, who was all
of seventeen, to spending all of their money on fancy
things. However, Tina hadn't seen a fancy thing in that
house the entire time she'd been their ward, only a
seemingly endless supply of dirty dishes and laundry
from their five small children.

"Soon, no one will look at you because you're
stuffing your mouth with cake, and you look like a pig."

Tina winced. That hurt. But the woman in question
only looked angry. She was young yet, and still had
some fight in her, Tina thought. Eventually, all of the
Mrs. Grangers became tired and empty.

More Spanish, a hand gesture, and then the woman
launched herself at the man.

There was a scuffle, as they were basically the same
shape and size. There was some yelling, but all of
Tony's male relatives quickly surrounded the combat-
ants. Tina released her grip on her phone. Her hand
hurt from how hard she'd been holding it.

*I'm not upset. I was just concerned that they
might ruin Emma's wedding memories, or Emma's*

wedding budget. So why was the cake rolling around in her stomach?

The phone rang. She jerked. It startled her out of her jumbled thoughts. She wasn't vulnerable. Not in any way. Not anymore.

"Hello?"

"Tina. Are you all right? You said there was a fight."

"Nothing major. Just two people who were supposed to care about each other, tearing each other apart verbally, and then having a go at it physically. Fortunately, Tony has a huge family and they just sort of engulfed them and carried them away."

"So why don't you come over? And bring some cake." His voice grew husky. "I want to eat it off your breasts, baby. We won't even need to get out the plates or the silverware."

It stirred her, but she resisted. "I don't think so. Not tonight."

Why even try? Tyler was not the kind of let-off-steam date she needed right now, no matter how hot he made her feel. And anything more than that was just a huge waste of her time. In ten years, they'd be yelling at each other or getting their own divorce lawyers. Hell, what was she thinking? They wouldn't last ten months.

"What's wrong?" he asked.

"Nothing. I just ate too much cake."

"Then I can help you work off those pesky calories," he coaxed.

"Thank you for that kind offer, but not tonight."

"Tomorrow? Remember I owe you lobster this weekend."

"I don't know."

"I go from being offered cake to being brushed off completely? That hurts, sweetheart."

"You can handle it. Check your little black book. I'm sure you can find someone to crack the lobster and then hand-feed it to you." *It just won't be me.*

"I don't give up that easily."

"It doesn't matter. It takes two to tango, so to speak, and I'm not interested."

"That's not the impression I got this morning."

"It was the influence of the wedding. It brought out the romantic in me and now I've seen the flip side to remind me of reality."

"That's not reality, but I'll let you bow out tonight because I don't like the sad tone in your voice."

"I'm not sad," she protested.

"Melancholy? Feeling your biological clock ticking?"

He sounded frustrated rather than combative. Still, she couldn't let it pass.

She nibbled her manicure, not sure how he'd take it if she pushed the boundaries. "My biological clock is only at the mercy of the nearest sperm bank. I don't need a man for anything—though I admit I may want one occasionally, since men still have sexual equipment that's better than anything that can be purchased on the Internet. At least for now."

"Are you challenging me?"

"If the shoe fits." Though he couldn't see, she lifted

one of her Yoyo Zeppa heels with the scarlet bottoms. Expensive shoes always reminded her that she'd made it out of the world she'd grown up in and was walking in a completely different place.

He chuckled. The sound was deep and sexy. He was not only a good sport, but also a kind man. A miracle. It almost unclenched the knots in her stomach. Almost. "I've got to go. I'm tired."

"Sweet dreams, sweetheart. I'll be thinking of you."

"I'll just bet you will." She snapped the phone shut with only a nibble of regret. *You're only missing out on the cream cake foreplay,* she told herself, *and you can do that anytime, with anyone.* Tyler might have been a nice change of pace, but it was time to get back to reality. She didn't do lawyers, even smothered in wedding cake.

THURSDAY AFTERNOON, Tina finished up early, changed out of her work clothes and then went out to run some errands. Later, she pulled up to the dilapidated house on Pomice Road in her little car, where it was definitely out of place. She didn't worry about it though, since she was under the protection of the local gang of street kids. A couple of hundred bucks bought a lot of protection in this neighborhood.

After fishing a mountain of grocery bags out of her trunk, she waddled up to the porch with her hands so full one of the women sitting on the porch had to open the screen door for her. The living room was full of threadbare couches. Three women and several children all sat listlessly in front of the blaring TV. Tina smiled, but none of the women smiled back. It didn't faze her; she kept going, familiar with the route, on her way to the heart of the home.

When she reached the kitchen, she put her bags up on the counter with a sigh. A large, round woman of Hawaiian descent caught sight of her from the hall and came running into the kitchen, beautiful, dark hair streaming behind her like a cloak.

Tina tried not to flinch as she was gathered up in the firm hug of Sammola Daton, main social worker and house mother of this particular women and children's shelter.

"Tina, I'm so glad you could come today."

"Why? What's up? You weren't very specific on the phone."

"We've got a situation. It's the new woman and her little boy. The husband might know where they are and apparently, he's on his way."

"And you didn't tell me? I went shopping, when I should have come right over!"

"What were you going to do? I called the police, and then I called you, but I wasn't gonna tell you it was an emergency and have you get into a wreck driving like a maniac to get here when we don't know anything for sure."

"So where are the police?"

"Apparently, it's been a rough day for Hank and his crew. Maybe it's the heat that's got so many people stirred up. The best they can do right now is to keep driving by. It's not a day when they can just come for the donuts." She made herself laugh.

Tina often thought Sam made herself laugh because it kept her sane, and because it made the terrible scar on her cheek disappear into the deep, beautiful dimples. The woman had once been terribly hurt by her spouse, but she'd turned her life around and become a psychologist with a master's degree in counseling.

"I guess the police can't just hang around. Who else could we get?" Tina admitted with frustration. "We need to hire someone for security."

"You know this place. The women are jumpy. I thought about bringing in one of my cousins. But they're all big like me, and I know of more than one gal who'd take the kids and run if a strange man hung around." Sam touched her cheek absently.

"Okay, so I'll just stick around for a little while. Maybe he's just blowing smoke. It's likely he'll just go off somewhere and get drunk. If not, we'll come up with a solution. Oh, I brought some stuff."

Sam's lovely smile shone. "Thank you. You always bring good stuff. Everyone eats well when you've been here."

"One of the things I always hated about places like this was the bland food. I swore they must have gotten the food in the tasteless aisle. Now I know starch is cheap," Tina said.

"So you'll stay for lunch?"

"And dinner. I'll even help you cook."

Sam looked at her slyly. "Does anyone else in the whole world know that you cook?"

"No way. I did enough dishes in other people's homes to last me a lifetime."

FROM WHERE he stood, deep on the darkened front porch, Tyler watched Tina looking sexy in her casual shorts and trademark high-fashion heels. So far, he'd managed to remain there unseen. He was mesmerized by the two very different women before him, and their poignant if matter-of-fact conversation, which he could hear through the screen door.

He'd never expected to learn so much about Tina when he'd called to bribe her assistant for her whereabouts. In fact, he'd been working on the assistant for weeks in hopes of learning as much about Tina as possible. Only the fact that the assistant was actually worried about Tina's safety today had made her admit Tina's whereabouts.

He watched through the screen door as Tina pulled some take-out boxes from the bags on the counter. If he couldn't get to her through flowers and fancy dates, maybe he could figure out what actually interested her. Who was she? Why was she at this shelter? Tina was a puzzle he'd been trying to solve since the cruise.

"You go, girl. I'd *only* do takeout if I could afford it." The larger woman smacked her lips and rolled her hips in a smooth circle as if she were dancing.

"I'm here to make your take-out dreams come true. I brought all of your favorites."

"You brought those little dumplings? I've died and gone to heaven. What is it about Chinese that makes a girl feel so spoiled?"

"After a hundred pounds of mac and cheese, anything else is heavenly. I can't tell you how many pots of those I scraped, and floors I scrubbed, for that matter. Not to mention children I bathed," Tina said.

"Yeah. We've always got plenty of children to bathe here, too, poor souls. Seems they always get the worst of it."

"I was no saint. I only bathed the children because I couldn't stand sleeping in the same room or bed with a dirty kid. Some of them fought it, but they got soaped up until they smelled good."

Tyler saw the determined little girl in the woman, and finally he knew The Shark had come first, before the sophistication. Somehow, a small girl had been tough enough to beat the system in the most spectacular way. He wanted to grab her in a giant hug, and most of all he wanted to tell her how amazing she was.

Only he didn't know how she'd react when she caught him prying. Should he reveal himself? What if she caught him? This time, she probably would blacken his eye or kick him in the balls. Damn Nelson for suggesting he spy on Tina as part of his plan to win her. The man always managed to get him in trouble.

"You'd better eat these before the kids see them," Tina prodded. "Sam, you're a marshmallow. You'd share."

"Built like one, anyway." Sam chuckled.

Tina shook her head as she popped a fried wonton into her mouth.

"Girl, I know you always had respect for yourself. How'd you do it?" The woman put her hands on her hips.

Tyler paused. What would she say? Tyler wondered. How had she ended up in foster homes anyway?

"I guess it was because I knew my parents just hadn't given me up. They died. It wasn't their fault. But that made it harder, too. No one was ever coming to rescue me. I had to do it myself." Tina put her hands on her hips, mirroring the other woman's attitude, and then she grinned.

"Apparently, I wasn't cooperative or cute enough. And I told the truth. No one likes that. So I got shifted pretty often. In a way it, was a blessing. Why would I want to stay?"

But pain threaded through her voice.

Tyler had never thought to hear anything but confidence and conviction in that voice. It shook him. He wanted to comfort her.

"We survived and look where we are now," Sam said. Then she chuckled. "Of course, I still don't understand why I'm here. At least you're a big-shot lawyer."

"You're here to save them. Even the ones who don't know they want to be saved."

"Honey, by the time they come here, all they want is a safe place to hide and three meals a day."

"Well, we've got enough here for a couple of meals." Tina grabbed a bag and began unloading it.

"Oh, my goodness. You really did bring all of my

favorites. Shame on you. What if I was on a diet?" The woman put her hands on her substantial hips again.

"Are you?" Tina asked drolly.

She laughed. "Naw, it's easier to keep the men away when you got a few extra pounds or else I'd have to be remindin' myself that I don't want no man."

"Yeah, I have to keep reminding myself of that, too."

"You want to talk about him?"

Tina shook her head. "Naw. I just wanna eat."

"We all want more pleasure and less pain. It's a tough old world." The larger woman put a wheel of cheese on the counter. "This looks good. The kids need real cheese. I'll organize the stuff and lock some of it up so we can distribute it fairly. We've got some odd ones right now."

"Hey, I've got an idea." Tina pulled herself up to sit on top of the kitchen counter. "Instead of cooking, let's order pizza from Riggelles. It's the best. Then the food I brought will last you longer."

"The kids will love it, but you know it's not in our budget," Sam warned. "And I've got a full house."

Tina smiled. "It's not a problem. Break out the phone book."

Tyler decided it was time to announce his presence. But how to do it without incurring Tina's wrath.

"What the hell do you think you're doing?"

The screeching from behind startled Tyler and he spun around to face a sunken, emaciated-looking woman.

"Get the hell away from our house. Men aren't supposed to be here." Spittle flew from her mouth.

The woman pushed past him into the house and then slunk into the kitchen, where she took a protective stance behind a large butcher block, looking like a feral cat caught out in the open.

Tyler put his hands up in a nonthreatening manner.

"Who is it?" Sam asked.

Tina didn't turn around as she was reading off her credit card number to someone on the phone. It seemed that hysterical women didn't faze her. Now he understood why.

When she caught sight of him, the large lady relaxed and smiled. "Well, he's not the one we're worried about, Arlene. He's much too pretty and fancy. If I had to guess, I'd say he's come about our lady lawyer." She opened the screen door and stood there sizing him up.

"He's a bastard. All men are bastards," the frightened woman snarled.

It struck a chord. Tina could look like that. She knew how to snarl. Where had she learned it? Not all of the foster homes had been good places, he imagined. What had the little girl suffered? Had pain forged her tough exterior? Did the need for justice come from a past full of alienation and helplessness?

He felt badly that he hadn't seen beyond the passionate woman to the complicated soul underneath.

And he imagined Tina preferred it that way. Did she wonder what a guy would do if confronted with that kind of past?

What will I do?

He entered the house, his hands open in front of him.

"I'm not a bastard, I'm just a lawyer," he told them. Then he deliberately directed his gaze at the smiling woman and away from the frightened one. "Although some people think they're one and the same thing."

"We get some of that around here. But it's better now that we got our famous lady lawyer."

"She *is* good. But not as good as I am."

She laughed. "I'm Sam, and I never argue with a lawyer."

"You sound like you're from the islands."

"Hawaii, mainly Oahu, and then here to Florida. I'm like a fish—I can't get too far from the ocean."

"You sound like gorgeous beaches and sunsets." He stuck out his hand. "I'm Tyler. Run away with me. Please."

"Tyler, honey, I'm tempted."

He dropped her hand as if she'd disappointed him. "But you're turning me down?"

"No, I'm thinking seriously about your offer."

She grinned and patted his shoulder in a consolatory way, but there was a line above her eyes telling him something was bothering her.

"Honey, what are you doing here? This isn't a good place for a man to be hanging out. Good thing you're dressed so pretty, otherwise the ladies might have clawed that handsome face of yours to shreds."

"You caught me. I snuck in to see Tina."

"That fancy lawyer lady thinks she's so important, bringing all that fancy food, buying stuff, but bringing him's against the rules. I know the rules. That bitch!"

"It's okay, Arlene. He's another lawyer who's gonna help us with Lisa and her little boy."

"Tyler, what are you doing here?"

Tina sounded so casual. Agreeable, really. No doubt it was the calm before the storm, because it wasn't like her. She didn't even look like herself except for the shoes. There was not a lick of makeup on her gorgeous face, and her hair was actually tied back in a ponytail. Maybe that was why he'd pictured her as a little girl as he'd watched her from the porch.

"Counselor, I asked you a question."

He breathed easier; she was going to be cool, whether it was due to Sam's presence or Arlene's he didn't know or care. "I saw you turn onto Connelly Street and I wondered if you would be okay on this side of town."

It was just a little lie. A social lie, really. So why did he feel guilty?

"I'm okay. You can leave now."

"I see."

"No, you don't see anything. This is a refuge and you're not welcome here."

"Yeah, when Lisa's husband shows up, he's gonna bloody her up and then your fancy face'll be next," Arlene was still spitting at him. "Just like my husband bloodied me. It's just the way things are unless you know where to hide. And Lisa deserves it because she didn't hide good enough."

Tyler had done enough research for clients to know that abused people were accustomed to certain behavior from those around them. Violence was comprehensible, and kindness often met with suspicion. So he ignored what he couldn't change and concentrated on something he might be able to do. "Who is Lisa?"

Tina came toward him with a too-sweet smile. "She's a client, and it's confidential. Go away. I'm handling it, counselor."

"Tina, wait." Sam seemed to be assessing him. "Tyler, can you handle yourself?"

"Yes. I can handle myself. I did some boxing in college."

Arlene hooted, grabbed a package of salami off the counter and then scooted out of the kitchen into yet another hallway. "I'm gonna enjoy watching the fancy-pants lawyer get his face kicked in. Yeah, I'm gonna enjoy it. Just like I enjoyed going a round with the fancy-pants lady lawyer who thinks expensive shoes will solve all of her problems."

"Arlene, don't start. We've been through this and we agree to disagree." Tina sounded almost weary.

"Just because you've got a law degree you think you're shi—"

"Enough!" Sam's voice cracked the air like a whip. "Let's concentrate on the problem at hand. Please, ladies."

Tyler watched Arlene slink out with a sense of relief. He didn't enjoy terrorizing women, although Sam certainly knew how to handle her.

"Lisa's man is like a gorilla and he's probably going to be high on top of everything. I don't want you to be a hero, but if he shows up maybe the three of us can keep him talking until the police arrive. I'd sure be grateful."

Tyler didn't look at Tina. "Can I lose the tie and have some pizza?"

"Honey, you sure can."

"I can handle Lisa's husband. We don't need Tyler," Tina protested.

"Girl, you might be good at fast talking but we need some man power. I wouldn't have gone looking for a civilian, but since he's a lawyer and already here in the house, he's the one."

Tyler watched Tina as she got the kitchen ready, and twenty minutes later retrieved the pizza from the delivery man. He helped as she spread a picnic blanket on the floor and then got everyone a plate and a drink. It was clear that she'd done such a thing before and some of the women even called her by name.

Tyler ate his pizza in silence, uneasy, and ignored by everyone but Sam.

Tina sat across the room with a little dark-skinned girl, obligingly picking the meat and anything that looked suspicious off her pizza. Tyler finally had the chance to question Sam.

"How long has Tina been working for the shelter?"

"I don't know. I get the impression she's before my time, and I'm going on three years."

"What do you know about her past?"

"What she told me about herself, she told me to win my respect. And I don't gossip."

Tyler smiled ruefully. "Can you give me some hints?"

"Why do you want to know, counselor?"

He winced at her tone. "Because she's about to eject me from her life, and I don't want to be rejected." He watched Tina stroke the little girl's dark braids with a tenderness he envied.

"I guess you like what you see."

"Passion and tenderness. Fight and flight. She'd be loyal, loving and fierce once she gave her heart away. And I'd never lack for a challenge. Yes. I like what I see very much. And I admire her mind—it's sharp and stimulating. She'd never bore me."

"And you're not interested in her body?" Samantha asked, mirth in her eyes.

"I'd have to be dead not to notice her body," he admitted.

"Why should I help you?"

"Because I have a lot to offer her."

"Arrogance. I like that in a man. It's probably why I always get into trouble."

She pushed her hair back from her face, apparently unselfconscious of her scar. Tyler thought the scar only made her face more compelling.

"Because the men I know have nothing to be arrogant about," she finished ruefully.

Tyler knew a guy with major attitude. True, he'd met the man when he was in trouble with the law, but it was for staging a protest on behalf of homeless people. He was actually a good guy who might appeal to a woman who appreciated an arrogant man.

Sam smiled, flashing her dimple, and tilting her

head toward him. "But you're different. Maybe you're good enough for my lady lawyer."

"I hope so."

"Try appealing to the child in Tina. I doubt she had much time to be a child."

"How do I do that?" He was truly puzzled.

"Make her laugh. Make her feel silly. Play with her. I'll bet you remember how to play, and I don't mean turn on the sports channel or get out your old baseball glove."

"What else *is* there?" Now he was truly baffled. "Video games?"

"The arcade might be fun. Challenge her. I'll bet she'd like the mini race cars, or a game of laser tag. My nieces and nephews love those places."

He could see them in the arcade, racing cars on the computer and then around the track. She'd gloat if she won and try harder if she didn't. It could be fun. He wondered if she played pool or foosball. "What else?"

"Give her silver helium balloons instead of roses. We got some here one time, and she looked enchanted by them."

"Balloons?" he asked doubtfully. He couldn't imagine Tina with balloons.

"How bad do you want to get close to her? Are you willing to work at it? It's not going to be easy to get her to open up to you like she does Chantel." She gestured toward the little dark-haired girl.

He looked over at Tina, who was obliviously

wrapped up in the child, Chantel. "And I don't think my hair is long enough to braid."

"Also, you have no bruises."

Tyler looked at Sam. "What kind of bruises?"

"No kind."

Tyler shook his head, at a total loss.

"You've got the perfect thing going. You look like you've walked out of a magazine. Now take that little girl— She's been through hell and that's made her more real than most people—definitely more real than the kids she hangs with. I think that's why she comes here. Can you prove you're real, too?"

"How the hell do I do that?" It was downright frustrating. First, he had to think of how to play with her and then he had to convince her that he was real?

Suddenly, Tina and the little girl burst out laughing.

It sounded so good to him. Could he do that? Could he make Tina laugh?

A thin scream came from the front room.

Sam looked up as if she knew instinctively what was happening beyond the room, and the expression on her face froze Tyler to the bone.

"You just might have your chance to show Tina what you got, and just how real you are."

The room split down the middle with some of the women and children going toward the back and others going toward the living room as if drawn to the violence they imagined was taking place there.

Tyler followed the exodus to the living room.

The man on the front porch looked exactly like

Tyler imagined, only sixty pounds heavier. Tyler sucked in his breath. This guy looked as if he could break him in two with one hand.

"Where's my little boy? I'm not going to hurt none of you, if you just hand over my little boy, Petie. My bitch wife had no right to take the boy. I didn't hit him much. A boy needs a little smacking around to keep him in line. I didn't do it too much."

Sam glided to the front of the crowd of women, who'd stopped about ten feet short of the front door.

"Now, Mr. Houser, you know you can't come in here because of the protective order from the court."

The man's face crumpled like he was going to cry and then it cleared. "No protective order is gonna stop a man from talking to his own son. That ain't right. It ain't."

"The police are on their way, and it's best if you just go home. Go home. You'll get to see your son. I'm sure it won't be too long."

Tyler remembered seeing Pete eating pizza with a cast on his arm and hoped it would be a long time indeed before the man was allowed to see his son. He folded his arms, kept his eyes on Tina and waited, leaning against the peeling wallpaper.

"I want my son, and no fat whore is going to tell me to wait. No one is going to tell me anything." The man reached for the doorknob.

Tina stepped forward. "What about a skinny whore who just happens to be Lisa's hard-assed lawyer? And who's gonna see you locked away for a good chunk of your miserable life if you so much as come one step inside that door?"

It was amazing, the way she faced him down. And the man actually hesitated. But Tyler was terrified for her, even though Tina sounded like she could chew the man up and spit him out.

Tyler and the intruder surged forward at the same time. Tyler placed himself in front of Tina, just as the big man put one huge foot through the screen door, which gave with a muted ripping sound.

Batting the screen material aside, the man looked up at Tyler, who knew what was coming the minute their eyes met. He tucked his head under his shoulder as the man came forward as if to mow him down.

When the man actually hit Tyler, he felt his teeth come together hard enough to send a spasm through his jaw. But somehow he stayed on his feet.

As the man began to pummel him, Tina and Sam attacked the man from behind with an arsenal Tyler hadn't noticed. Tina had a rolling pin, and Sam a baseball bat she obviously had some experience swinging.

Then the huge man caught Tyler in the shoulder and sent him spinning off balance. He could feel it in his bones.

Everyone was yelling for the man to stop. He didn't. His failing arms caught Tyler again, as he attempted to right himself. This time the blow caught Tyler across the face and threw him to the floor with a thump. He opened his eyes to a matted shag carpet in faded, puke green. Either it was the carpet or the blow to the eye that was making him queasy. Did that prove he was real?

"Tyler? Are you okay?"

The real fear in Tina's voice had him struggling to his feet. He was no hero. In fact, he was losing this fight spectacularly. But with Tina and the other women in danger, he had to try.

He grunted as he struggled to his feet. Through tearing eyes he assessed the situation.

Tina was threatening the man from one side, and Sam was at the other side with the bat cocked as though she meant to hit a homer. A dark mark bled across her cheek, the smooth one.

Tyler felt a red tide of anger he'd never experienced. He'd be damned if he was going to let a psychotic side of beef hurt Sam again.

"Jimmy, just go away," a voice pleaded from behind them.

"Give me my son!" The man foamed at the mouth like a rabid dog. His eyes were wild, and his fists kept flailing at no apparent target.

Tyler knew he had to get behind the man and try to take him down at the knees. He looked around for something to distract Jimmy but didn't see anything so he looked at the front door behind the man, pointed and shouted, "Hey, kid, run away. Go now!"

Jimmy turned abruptly, and Tyler took that moment to drop down and roll into the back of Jimmy's knees, expecting Jimmy to fall, and fall hard. Unfortunately, Jimmy only stumbled. Tyler groaned and grabbed a huge foot, cursing when he got stepped on, but grappling with the foot. The man stumbled again but somehow stayed on his feet.

"Petie," he roared.

Tyler sucked in a breath as the man dragged him into an old wooden piece of furniture that felt a lot more solid than it looked. He knew his ribs would be bruised to hell in the morning.

Then the man reached down and grabbed Tyler's face in both of his huge hands, and Tyler knew this was going to hurt.

TINA WANTED to rip Jimmy's face off with her nails. Tyler was down, and the man looked as if he was going to crack his head like a melon. She did the only thing she could think of, as the man bent over Tyler. She kicked out, trying to catch Jimmy in the crotch and incapacitate him. But apparently, she missed because Jimmy only grunted and proceeded to bang Tyler's head on the carpet.

Sam yelled and brought the bat down on Jimmy's shoulder. He yelled louder, but still didn't let go of Tyler.

Tina grabbed his greasy hair and pulled, using all of her weight as leverage. As she felt the give of the hair, the giant screamed. At that moment Tyler landed a fist in Jimmy's face. Then those huge hands came at her….

"Freeze. It's the police. Everyone put your hands on your heads."

There was a soft sound, a click. Tina didn't recognize the sound, but obviously the giant did.

The big man immediately froze.

Tina looked up and saw that one cop had drawn his gun on them, and the other had a Taser ready.

"Officer Haverty. I'm so happy to see you," Tina said matter-of-factly.

The cop smiled crookedly, never taking his eyes off the giant. "Almost didn't recognize you, Miss Henderson, but I'm glad to be of service. Is that our own Mr. Walden lying on the carpet?"

"Yes, and he's glad to see you, too."

"He would be glad if he could actually see," Tyler ground out. His eye pounded where Jimmy had hit him and his head was thrumming a different beat. He felt like shit.

Jimmy just stood, hands on his head, waiting as if he'd been switched off, apparently respecting the firepower of the police as he respected no person.

"We're well acquainted with Jimmy. There's a protective order, and I'm guessing he's just violated it. You know where you're going, Jim. Just leave those hands on your head and get on your knees."

"I just wanted to see my boy," the man whined as they cuffed him and then hauled him to his feet.

Tina reached down to help Tyler stand up. He looked awful. "My hero," she told him. And because he looked so pathetic she reached up and gave him a gentle kiss on his undamaged cheek. He seemed much taller without her usual heels. Or perhaps it was his heroics that made him seem so tall.

"*You* saved me. Do you know how embarrassing that is?" he complained.

"That's because I'm a modern woman." She pulled away in order to get a good look at his face. "Wow, you're going to have an incredible shiner tomorrow."

"I think he dislocated my shoulder." He sat down on one of the couches, rubbing his shoulder. "I could sure use a hot shower and a massage."

Tina sighed. Leave it to him to try to take advantage of the situation. The man was a menace even with that goofy look on his puffy face and his normally perfect hair standing on end.

One of the police officers immediately turned attentively to help Tyler. Of course, it was the female officer. Tina curled her lip in disgust as the woman gently examined him and then pronounced him only bruised, but offered to call him an ambulance if he would prefer a professional opinion.

Tina waited with her arms crossed over her heart. *I'm not jealous. I'm just impatient. The man's worthless. He almost got killed because he couldn't handle himself.*

But even as she thought it she knew she was being unfair.

Sam giggled a little, but it was laced with hysteria as she looked around at her ladies. "I guess we lost the magazine rack and the bookshelf when Tyler was getting thrown around like a bowling ball. Otherwise, everyone's okay," she stated.

As if they'd been given permission the women started whispering amongst themselves.

"I suppose you expect me to replace those things?" Tyler asked from the couch where the policewoman still hovered over him. "Would it make me more real if I tell you that not only am I going to replace the furniture, but I'm going to buy you brand-new wall-to-wall carpet, as my close encounter with your present carpet wasn't very pleasant?"

"Show-off," Tina told him.

"Yeah, it makes you about as real as it gets," Sam told him, and then she laughed and walked over to lean on Tina.

"Don't laugh," Tina muttered, nudging Sam with her elbow. "Don't you see he's busy flirting with the policewoman? And 'more real'? What the hell is that supposed to mean? He just wants to score points by buying new carpet. Then you won't remember that he ate it on the old carpet. He's pathetic."

Tina bent to pick up the spilled magazines, wishing she'd offered to replace the carpet, which was truly hideous. *I guess I just thought it was supposed to be awful, since it always was in every shelter I ever visited.*

"Let Tyler show off, as long as my girls get new carpet out of it. Men need you to make a fuss over them. Especially when their ego's been damaged by a head pounding."

"Too bad it didn't knock any sense into him." Tina brushed a worried hand over Sam's darkening cheek. "You need some ice for this."

"Don't you worry about it. I've had worse and your man, he came through."

"He's not my man, and he just got the hell beat out of him." She was beginning to feel her own bruises from where Jimmy's thrashing arms had caught her. "What do you think happened to Jimmy's wife and kid?"

"She's probably coaxing Pete out of hiding right now. I told her beforehand which closet to stash the kid in if Jimmy showed up."

"I wish we'd hired professional security." Tina rubbed her arms.

"We did fine with a little help from Tyler."

Tina could almost still hear the hollow thud of his head being beaten against the carpet. "I guess Tyler did well enough." She watched as the policewoman moved away from him and then reluctantly followed the other officers out the front door. Tina thought she hesitated and was sure the woman looked back at Tyler.

"Honey, we all did well enough. Even the ladies kept it together better than I anticipated."

"You really need some ice," Tina repeated.

"I'll take care of it. You go and make Tyler feel like a hero. That's all that policewoman was doing. A man isn't like a girl. He's gotta have his ego stroked."

"If Tyler's ego gets any bigger, it won't fit inside his head." But she reluctantly walked over to the couch and then settled down beside him, surprised to feel her legs quivering. "Wow, that was wild."

"I might have a concussion," he complained. "I have a huge headache."

"Your head's too hard to break." But she thought he might be right. He'd taken some significant abuse.

"I need someone to stay with me tonight and wake me up every few hours with kisses," he said, deadpan.

She grinned. Obviously, he wasn't that badly off. "With kisses? Was that the policewoman's professional opinion?"

"Lots of kisses."

"Anything else?"

"You should say nice things about my courage, strength and manly honor."

She leaned against him, gently. "You were very heroic and wonderful today. Thank you."

He touched the side of her face. "Can you look me in the eye and say that? I really need to hear it because I'm looking at Sam's bruise, and I know he caught you with his fists. You probably hurt as much as I do."

Tina took a steadying breath, glad to be in one piece, other than the bruise on her shoulder where Jimmy had pushed her aside. She turned to Tyler and looked directly into his blue, blue eyes. "Today, you're my hero. I didn't expect you to take on a man built like a WWE wrestler all by yourself."

"Will I still be your hero tomorrow?"

She choked out a laugh. "Don't push your luck."

"Will you watch over me tonight?" Water trickled from his swollen eye.

She knew she'd never sleep worrying about him anyway. "Okay."

"Will you go out with me this weekend?"

She sighed. "Yes. I owe you."

"Will you marry me?"

This time she pushed him away. "You are such an opportunist!"

Grinning like a little boy, face all swollen and lopsided, he leaned forward and gave her a peck on the cheek. "I always take advantage when I'm on a roll. It's too bad you don't have a concussion, or you might have said yes."

"So it's the concussion speaking?"

"Of course, or the shame. What man in his right mind wouldn't propose to a woman who just saved him from sure death on a dirty carpet in front of twenty witnesses?"

"I can see your point, even if you're not making sense."

He stroked her face. "I may not be making sense, but I'll be content if you stay nearby." He seemed to sag against the back of the couch. "And I'll pledge my undying love if only you'll get me some sort of pain reliever, extra strength. Did you happen to have a steak in one of those grocery bags? Or some ice?"

Concerned by the pained look on his face, Tina got up to get the medication. At the doorway, she turned to look back. A few of the women were huddled around him. He might look like hell, but he was definitely heroic, and any woman would be proud to have him pledge his undying love.

Any woman except her.

She just hoped he'd realize it when he was more coherent.

6

TINA FOUND HERSELF being a very unlikely nursemaid to a cranky patient and two sympathetic, clingy dogs. "Tyler, would you just lie down, and go to sleep! You're driving both me and these dogs crazy."

"I'm walking it off." A table nearly tipped over as he tried to walk around it, using it to hold him up. The lamp on top of it wobbled as precariously as he did. Ray shrank down into his doggie cushion, apprehensive, and Frosty almost got his tail stepped on as Tyler abruptly changed direction.

"Stumbling it off, is more like it. You look like you've had too much to drink." She hoped if he was going to go down he'd fall on the plush carpet in the middle of the room. It would be a lot less messy that way if he landed on his face, which seemed likely.

The Oriental rug was still rich with years of color. He'd matched it beautifully with dark cherry leather couches, and forest-green and black accents. His place reflected warmth, rather than the money he'd no doubt spent on the beautiful one-of-a-kind pieces.

She sucked in a breath as he almost knocked down

a stylized sculpture. "Sit down before you break some-thing!" she snapped. "You don't have a lick of sense. Doesn't it hurt to walk?"

He stopped and looked at her as if *she* were crazy. It made her cover her mouth to suppress a giggle because his normally perfect hair was standing on end, and that blackened eye glowed with what might have been desire, but she was pretty sure was the result of a hammering headache.

"Why won't you settle down?" she asked more gently. After all, she owed him some patience after he'd taken a beating for her sake. "Tyler?"

Pushing his hair back from his face he finally turned to her. "Why won't I settle down? I've finally got you where I've wanted you for months, and I can't think. It's humiliating, and all I can think about is how I got the crap kicked out of me, and in front of all those women, and now I ache all over. It's like a brief that's just not coming together. I know once I find the angle I need, I'll be able to convince the jury, but so far all I'm doing is going over it and over it in my head." He looked around as if he wasn't really sure what he wanted to do.

He put his hands on his head. "God has the most amazing sense of humor. You've been driving me crazy since the cruise. Now that I've got you where I want you, I'm not at my best."

"You're repeating yourself," she said absently then added drily, "And I'm not sure I've ever seen you at your best. Just get horizontal and sleep so the rest of us can settle down." She gestured toward the dogs.

"Never seen me at my best, huh? What about on the cruise, and as The Bandit stripper. I remember being pretty good at that. If I recall correctly, you begged for us to get horizontal," he said somewhat smugly.

Feeling a little flare of heat at the thought of him as The Bandit, and only a little irritated at his presumption, she wriggled on the surface of the stool she'd pulled up to the bar. "I wouldn't be making plans to take it on the road just yet if I were you."

"Are you saying you wouldn't like a repeat? I've still got all of the stuff."

She took a cleansing breath. *I'm not aroused.* There was no way she could make demands on his body right now. She'd kill him in the condition he was in. "Okay, so your brains appear to be intact. But it's your brawn that's suffering. Go to bed!"

Sinking down on the couch, he looked so defeated it gave her an uncomfortable ache in the vicinity of her heart.

Don't be silly. I haven't got a heart. She nibbled her nail.

He sank back against the cushions. "Can you promise me something?" he asked with his eyes closed.

"What?" she asked suspiciously.

"Will you promise to come back here at a more auspicious time? Please? I'd like to make dinner and sit down on the couch together. I want to see you walk around barefooted, and then I want to take your beautiful feet into my hands and rub them." He paused for a moment as if collecting his thoughts. "Maybe we can even play a board game."

"A board game?" Tina didn't know what the hell he was thinking. "Do you mean you have a board game like strip poker or something?"

Smiling an innocent smile he replied, "Naw, I was thinking Scrabble. I'll bet you've got killer instincts when it comes to board games."

"I don't know. I've never had much of a chance to play them," she said, bemused at the turn the conversation had taken. "Are board games dating milestones in your repertoire? Strip poker, I could imagine. And I'm really good at poker. I'll have you stripped down to your skin just as soon as you're feeling better."

She looked him over. He'd feel more comfortable if he got out of his constrictive clothing. Those jeans hugged him like a lover. Only she didn't dare put her hands on him right now.

She definitely felt revved. For some reason, the violence at the house had affected her. Or maybe it had been his attempt to champion a bunch of misfit women. Whatever the cause, the effect had her libido humming.

"Are you falling asleep on that couch?" She hoped he was, as he'd be much safer from her wicked intentions.

"I guess so." He yawned. "I feel wasted."

"I'm not surprised. He got you good."

"I guess I didn't impress you much," he said sheepishly. Frosty jumped up against the side of the couch, whining for attention, and he patted the puppy absently. "I'm okay, boy."

She stood up and then came around to sit on the thick wooden coffee table in front of his couch, keeping a safe distance between them. Safe for *him*. "I guess you did all right back there."

Frosty transferred his attention to her, ecstatically licking her fingers.

Glaring at the pup out of one eye, Tyler growled, "Traitor dog."

"Frosty's just covering all his bases. He doesn't know who's going to feed him tonight."

"He already ate like a pig this afternoon. Really, there's nothing for you to do except give me the TLC I've got coming as the champion of the hour."

"One minute you're embarrassed and the next you're the champion. Why don't you add brave, wonderful and strong to your list?"

He focused on her and she leaned in close enough to see that his pupils were equally dilated in the light.

"Do you really mean it?"

"Which part?"

"That I was heroic, wonderful, brave and strong?" He patted the couch beside him. "Come and tell me all about it, up close and personal."

Ray looked up from his bed on the floor and then lay down with a deep doggy sigh.

Sighing herself, mostly for effect, she moved to sit beside him. "You were all of those admirable things," she said magnanimously.

She just wanted him to feel strong and well so she could have her wicked way with him. That was all.

This praise was purely for effect. She couldn't help it. He affected her. Even disheveled and pathetic, she found him totally sexy and attractive. Boy, was she crazy or what?

"Thank you," he told her. "You're right. I should take it easy. I'm going to take off my shoes and just relax here in your loving arms." He added innocently, "You can even rub my feet with the peppermint lotion that I'd planned to use on you."

"I'm not the one with the concussion, so there's no way you're going to sell me on rubbing your feet," she told him drolly. "Never in a million years."

He scooted closer to her, almost leaning against her.

Shrugging, she slid to the farthest end of the couch. "I'd be happy to give you a gift certificate for a massage from a friend of mine at the spa. He'll make you weep with gratitude when he's done with you."

Tyler scooted closer, pinning her legs to the couch with his shoulders and then putting his head in her lap.

Her body started humming. He was right there between her legs. She bit her lip. "I'm not going to be your pillow for very long," she warned him.

"Just stay here with me for a few minutes." His eyes closed. "Please?"

The pup jumped up against the side of the couch again. She petted him until he flopped back down.

"How are you doing?" She didn't know if she was talking to the pup, Tyler, or herself. Looking into Tyler's damaged face she felt real regret. *He'll be fine.*

The bruising wasn't too deep, and she'd seen lots

of bruises in her time, both on her body and others. Corporal punishment had been a favorite of her foster fathers, who apparently didn't know their own strength. Fortunately, she's never been beaten excessively. No broken bones or a broken spirit. Some kids weren't so lucky.

Tentatively, she reached out and smoothed down his hair. He sucked in a breath.

"Am I hurting you?" she asked anxiously.

"No." This time it was a sigh. "It feels heavenly. Like an angel touched me."

She stroked him again. "Don't be so damn dramatic."

"I can't help it."

She put a finger on the red streak across his cheekbone. "You should be worried more about your face and less about your ego."

"You could kiss it."

"Don't push your luck," she said darkly.

"Tell me about the places where you grew up."

"What?"

"The homes you grew up in, were they like the shelter?"

She could hear the underlying hint of sympathy that she always tried to avoid. Years ago, when she used to make the mistake of unveiling a little of her past to people she knew, they would avidly ask for details. Were you an abused child? Did you get sexually molested? Did you feel unloved? Is that why you're so determined to succeed?

And though she realized none of those questions

were exactly unreasonable—since she'd long ago asked some of them of herself—she hated the feeling of vulnerability. She always felt as if she'd been caught out in public naked or at least without a pair of four-hundred-dollar shoes.

She knew exactly why she spent so much money on the shield of her clothing. But she'd never admitted to anyone. "What do you want to know?"

At their feet, Frosty whimpered as if he sympathized with her.

"I don't know. What did you dream about when you were under the covers and hidden away from the real world? I always felt as if there was nothing in the world that could hurt me as I relaxed into sleep, even the green monster under my bed."

"You had one of those, too?" She grinned. He was so sweet, and seemed kinda sleepy himself, maybe half in a safe place right now. How could she take offense? "I imagined that I was in a cocoon and that when I woke up I'd be able to fly away to another place on strong, beautiful wings."

Oh, God, where had that come from?

He turned on his side and snuggled closer.

She let him, pulling the throw from the back of the couch over his shoulders.

"That's a sweet thought, and you did it. I've yet to see a more beautiful butterfly."

She looked down at her ratty clothing, dusty from rolling around on thirty-year-old carpet. "I think that's because you have your eyes closed."

"Naw, I've got them wide open, and I see a woman sitting on the floor with a blanket spread out in front of her having a carpet picnic with a bunch of frightened women and kids. She's hugging a little girl and picking all of the unwanted stuff off her pizza. The little girl is looking at her the way I feel, like she's the most beautiful woman in the whole world."

"That little girl doesn't know any better, and you've got a concussion. You'd better not say anything you'll regret. If you get maudlin and ask for my hand in marriage again, I'll sue you for breach of contract and you'll regret it."

"I don't think I'd regret anything."

She absently ran her fingers through his thick, soft hair. "I guess you're not going to lose much of this when you get older, it's so thick."

"Good genes." He wriggled. "Will you stretch out so I can put my feet up?"

The couch was wide and long so she scooted back against a large, thick pillow, reclining. He immediately put both his head and his feet up.

"Ah, did you mean to put your head back in my lap?"

"It feels better when you stroke me. Now I know why Frosty gets limp with ecstasy when I rub him."

"Very funny." But she continued to stroke him, feeling herself relaxing as she hadn't for a long time.

"Isn't this good?" he sighed.

"Yeah, it's okay. Go to sleep so I can go home."

"You have to stay the night and check on me. I think

you're supposed to wake me every three hours and make sure I'm coherent."

"You're not coherent now." A little sense of panic wrapped around her throat. "Don't you have a friend who can come over? I'm not too great at nursing."

"I can't tell any of my guy friends I got my ass kicked. Nelson will never let me forget it. It's too humiliating."

"Sometimes this friend thing is more trouble than it's worth."

"You don't mean it." His voice sounded thick.

He was falling asleep and fighting it. She slowed her rubbing and spread it out over the sides of his head.

He roused a little. "You do know how to love people."

She stopped her fingers, and then those fathomless blue eyes popped open. Even upside-down, he saw way more than was comfortable. She resumed rubbing. "Relax, you can psychoanalyze me tomorrow when you're feeling better."

"I just wanted you to know that I know how to love, too. I wouldn't let you down if I loved you."

It should have scared her to death.

"It would be crazy to love The Shark."

"Then I definitely qualify, especially at the moment." He did look crazed as he looked at her from upside-down, slitted, reddened eyes. "Stay and watch over me tonight?" His eyes slipped shut. "Please."

She curled her arms around his head on one side, and his shoulder on the other. Then she drew the cover over both of them. The dogs looked settled in for the duration and the lights were low enough to be comfortable. She let her eyelids droop.

"Maybe," she whispered, knowing that she lied. She would stay because it was the responsible thing to do. But only because of that.

He thought she knew how to love. But she didn't have a clue.

MORNING FOUND Tina wrapped in the smell of coffee and celery-green sheets. Abruptly, she sat up, tangled in the T-shirt she wore. Blinking, she settled back and tried to sort out her impressions of the night.

Eventually, she'd had to wake Tyler, as most of her body had gone to sleep with him lying in her lap. Somehow, she'd managed to steer him into the bedroom and she'd set her phone alarm for three-hour intervals. Then she'd crashed beside him as the couch had seemed too far away.

He'd been lucid enough each time she'd awakened him, although moody and cranky. Once she'd yelled back at him and told him it was all his fault for following her to the shelter. She'd never intended to get him mixed up in her problems.

She yawned. Time to get moving. She was already late to the office, although she'd left a long message for her assistant on voice mail. Maybe she'd make it an early evening.

"I guess you're tired," Tyler said from the doorway.

"I guess so." She smiled. His eye was truly spectacular. He was going to get so much shit from the people at the office, not that he didn't deserve it for meddling. "You've got a real impressive shiner there."

He put a hand up to his face. "Yeah, I expect to get a lot of sympathy from every woman I meet today. It's going to be amazing."

"Is that right?" Her mood instantly turned sour as she remembered how the policewoman had fawned on him. "I guess you'll enjoy being the hero of the day."

He came and sat down on the edge of the bed. "Thank you for staying."

She pulled the covers up to her chin though she wasn't cold. "It was the least I could do since you saved my butt."

"And what a pretty butt it is." He looked at her as if he wanted to have her for breakfast.

"Knock it off." She pushed her hair out of the way. "We've got to go to work."

When he looked to protest she continued. "Where you'll be everyone's hero. It should make for scintillating conversation."

"Of course, I'll make sure everyone knows the guy was six foot eight and weighed three hundred pounds. You won't go raining on my parade and tell everyone I was a wimp, will you?"

Reaching out to push the hair off his face, she told him, "If you're equally discreet. I don't remember covering myself in glory."

"And you remember your promise to see me?"

"I'm not the one who had brain damage. I remember. But you have to leave me alone to get some work done until tomorrow night. I don't like to be crowded."

"Like this?" He leaned in toward her, his face close enough for her to smell coffee and mint on his breath. "I love the way you look in my bed."

"Can I have some of that coffee?" she negotiated.

"Can I have a kiss?"

"Don't push your luck, mister. I stayed, I pampered, so now I'm taking the coffee and I'm heading home. No regrets, no looking back."

"Only looking forward to Saturday at eight?"

"Okay." She sighed. "But don't get any long-term ideas. Remember, I don't do relationships."

"I can't remember anything. I've got this massive headache."

Tina glared at him.

"I'll get you some coffee." He got up and left the room.

Adjusting her thong for maximum coverage, Tina climbed out of bed and into her jeans. It was long past time to make a run for it. This sort of cohabiting just wasn't right for her, no matter how comfortable it felt.

He came in and handed her the coffee, looking disappointed that she'd dressed. "Don't you like it black?"

"Sometimes."

"Do you live to confuse me?"

"I live to do as I please. It's a good approach because it's impossible to truly please another person."

"You could please me."

She looked him dead in the eye, and then handed him back the coffee cup. "No way in hell."

TYLER WATCHED her sexy little saunter as she exited out his bedroom, and his life. Again. It was getting to be a habit and he hated the way it made him feel.

He collapsed on the bed where she'd been lying, crawling up onto the pillow in order to catch a whiff of her perfume. He hadn't been kidding about the massive headache, but he'd been loath to show any more weakness around her.

She was so strong, so defensive. She was like a castle set up to withstand any siege. Putting his hands up to his sore face he groaned. None of this was going the way he'd imagined when he'd spent time with her on the cruise. He'd never had this much trouble getting a woman interested.

And he knew that this time he'd stay interested.

Always.

And not because Tina was challenging, multifaceted and amazing, all of the qualities he thought he'd need in a woman, but also because she was vulnerable, sensitive and generous.

Something magical happened to him when she walked into a room, and a part of him died when she walked away.

He sighed. He must have sustained brain damage. His entire life was upside-down. But then he'd felt like this before he'd gone those rounds with Jimmy. He'd felt like this since he'd taken her in his arms, dancing with her on the cruise. That night he'd fallen in love. Only he hadn't exactly recognized the emotion. It wasn't one he'd felt before.

So what was he going to do now? The plan wasn't going well. She should have fallen in love with his heroic rescue at the shelter, but obviously had not.

Now, his only hope was the advice Sam had given him, and he couldn't imagine a hard woman like Tina going down for the count just because he brought her some helium balloons. They were the strangest ammunition he'd ever heard of in a romantic siege. But he didn't have much choice. Flowers, tickets, getting the hell beat out of him, even a puppy hadn't softened her much.

Only sex seemed to bring out her softer side. So he would use that to lure her closer.

He rolled over, carefully. He wanted more amazing sex, but that wasn't all he wanted. He wanted her to need him all the time, not just when she was on the verge of an orgasm.

He wanted her to promise that she would return to him every time she walked away. Instead, she hadn't even bothered to look back.

7

AS SHE SAT in the waiting area of the restaurant, she chewed at a rough spot on her nail. Then she had to dig out her file because she'd simply made it worse.

She sighed. It was a crime to even own a file when she spent a fortune on her manicure every week. It was nerves. The man made her nervous, and that made her irritable and angry and fidgety. She'd picked up the phone several times to cancel their dinner but she knew what he'd say, what he'd do. He'd challenge her somehow.

Because she'd promised.

But she wouldn't go out with him again after tonight. It was silly to get upset—it was just a date, and in a public place. Did he even remember the comments they'd made about what was supposed to happen beneath the white tablecloth?

Surely not.

The file slid smoothly into her small manicure set, which fit perfectly inside a pocket of her briefcase. Organization was the key: staying focused, keeping on track, remembering what was important. She looked down at her brazen, brand-new Christian Louboutin shoes to reassure herself.

Why did she want him again, anyway? It had to be a residual effect of The Bandit thing because he shouldn't have kept her attention for this long. *I should just get a fur rug, some leather strips and another lover. That would do the trick.* Apparently, she had a faux fur and leather fetish.

I've had him all mixed in with a fantasy and then I felt sorry for him. That's all.

She pushed her hair back.

Looking up, she saw Tyler come through the ornate glass doors, looking carelessly casual and so gorgeous she felt her stomach contract.

I'm just hungry.

"I'm not late," he protested.

"No, you're not late." *I'm just in a hurry to get this over with.*

The hostess approached them. "Mr. Walden, your table is ready. Please come with me."

Tina turned to Tyler. "What's this? Not only did you manage to get a table, but you get the red-carpet treatment. Did you represent the owner of the restaurant in a food poisoning case or something?"

"No. I'm just a guy with connections out to impress the most beautiful lawyer lady in Florida."

"Thank you." A low level of anxiety had her nerves humming, but she didn't feel bad. No, she felt on, like she did when she finally had the angle and was ready to woo a jury with a knockout closing argument.

However, the closing argument didn't usually cause a knot of desire in the pit of her belly.

Don't think about it. Think about something else.

She looked around her. She'd fallen in love with the elegant restaurant from the moment she'd stepped inside. It was like a fairy garden from a production of *A Midsummer Night's Dream* with vivid, life-sized, ceramic animals peaking out from behind lush plants. Because the play had been the first live performance she'd ever been to, she'd always remembered its magic. The restaurant reproduced that feeling; she thought at any moment she might see Puck sneaking around a chair with a naughty grin on his face. The elegant furniture and the snow-white linen just blended into the motif.

"I like the frog," she confided as they walked by a four-foot frog whose face looked very human. "He's really a prince in disguise."

Tyler reached for her hand, and she let him hold it.

The hostess had to stop and step aside to let other guests come through a narrow aisle.

Tyler leaned close to her in an intimate fashion. "What else are you thinking about, besides frog princes?" He grinned like a naughty schoolboy. "I hope I don't qualify."

"You definitely qualify," she teased. "The frog bandit."

"Tonight, I intend to treat you like a princess."

"Just don't put me on a pedestal. I'd rather you treated me like a regular woman." But she was touched.

What the hell was wrong with her?

She needed to change the subject, quickly, before she got as sappy as Emma, who kept calling from her honeymoon. Jeez, it must be all the gushy stuff in her life that had her feeling so strange.

Mush. Mush. Mush. She must be sick or something.

A table on the other side of the bridge caught her eye. "Oh, look. It's somebody's birthday." She didn't mean to sound wistful, so she immediately tensed up, drumming her fingers on her briefcase "It's probably for a child. The kid will be thrilled."

"Why do you say so?" he breathed in her ear.

"Look at all the balloons and the flowers. It's so festive and beautiful."

"It's for you."

She blinked back sudden tears. No. She would not cry for a dozen slivery balloons bobbing from a centerpiece full of bright flowers.

The table was for four, but set intimately for two. It was the gorgeous centerpiece that took up all of the room on the table.

"Why would you do this?" She felt so giddy.

His smile was brighter than the profusion of flowers. "To please you."

She couldn't keep up the facade. She didn't know why, but her usual dignified facade cracked wide open. "I love it. It's wonderful. Thank you so much."

He nodded at the hostess. "We'll need your finest champagne, please."

Then he held the chair out for Tina. "Please have a seat. I intend to spend the evening spoiling you."

She scooted into the chair then pulled self-consciously at her dress. The thin material clinging to her figure so lovingly had seemed perfect when she'd thought seduction was the theme of the evening. And she'd worn garters with her stockings. Nothing more.

But now Tina was confused. He simply wanted to make her happy. Nothing was what she'd thought it would be. "I'm so surprised."

She looked up at the balloons glinting in the light. "Do I get to take them home?" She put her hand up to her mouth. She sounded like such an idiot. Where had that come from?

"I would love for us to take them home."

He looked at her with a hunger she couldn't mistake. It made her more comfortable with the situation. Desire, she understood. Roses, wine, and expensive chocolates all said a man wanted sex. Sex was easy.

But what did balloons say? For a moment, she'd been confused. Thank goodness his face said it all.

Just concentrate. The man wants sex. And the fact he's brought you balloons is just a bonus.

He seated himself beside her, brushing up against her leg in his elegant silk pants. The black shirt that went with them turned his eyes an impossible shade of blue. Tina couldn't help but think this was exactly what she'd had in mind for the evening. She reached out for his hand under the table and brought it to her naked knee.

Tyler went dead still. "Are you wearing garters?" he breathed.

"Yes. Just for you."

"I don't know if I'll get through the dinner without throwing you down on the table and ravishing you."

He made her feel warm and tingly. "That's a lovely thought, but what will it do to our distinguished reputations?"

"To hell with our reputations." He raised his water glass in one hand while the other made seductive circles on her knee.

"Why don't we just keep the seduction under the table? It's safer." She put her hand on his lap. He was already hard as a rock.

"Ah…"

She stroked him. He felt so firm under the smooth silk.

Just then three waiters descended on them with champagne, crab cakes and oysters. A hot loaf of herb bread set directly in front of her should have made her mouth water, but it was the feel of Tyler under the table making her hungry.

He spoke to the waiters, but it seemed he wasn't as articulate as usual. Tina smirked a little at the effect she was having on him. She stroked a little, eased up so he didn't ruin those beautiful pants, and then stroked a little more. For once, she felt totally in control of their relationship.

Until Tyler's hand stroked her as boldly as she'd stroked him. She sucked in a breath.

"Payback, sweetheart."

The waiter handed them each a glass of champagne. Tyler had to take his hand out from under the table, and

Tina wasn't sure if she was disappointed or relieved. After all, the evening was young.

He held out his glass.

"Are we celebrating?" she asked.

"We're celebrating the fact that no one was killed on Thursday."

She touched her glass to his and then sipped. The golden liquid felt as if it evaporated on her tongue. The bottle probably cost close to five hundred dollars. "This is wonderful, but it must have hurt your wallet."

"Not at all. I want to please you." He took a sip from his glass. "Whatever happened to our friend Jimmy, by the way?"

"He's in custody because you stopped him." That was laying it on a bit thick, as he'd just basically gotten in the way of the man's ham-sized fists, but it had taken courage to step between a huge, angry man and a bunch of defenseless women. Apparently, Tyler had depth. It had been a little disconcerting. She'd felt fear for him at the time and then actual tenderness afterward. Or close to tenderness. Not like her at all. "You were very courageous. He could have seriously messed up your face."

Tyler faced her with the black eye showing. It made the blue so intense. For a moment she dove into those eyes, staring, barely breathing, trying to decipher the man inside. Then she shook herself. *What am I doing?*

Her hand slid back into his lap. Sex was safer.

"I don't think my face was the issue. Who is representing Lisa?"

"Don't worry, she's in good hands."

"Tina, you don't have to take on everyone at the shelter. I can get some other lawyers to help. Everyone at the firm does a certain amount of pro-bono work, and it's a great cause. And now's the time to rope them in to help. The eye is all they can talk about. Since I've been teased so excessively, they owe me. Big-time."

She leaned forward, his scent filling her senses. "Are you sure you can get some of your colleagues to take cases? It would certainly speed things up. I've got three ladies who shouldn't be waiting—they need to get out of pretty desperate situations. Unfortunately, the longer it takes and the more red tape they have to wade through, the more likely they are to lose hope, and some of them even go back. They figure living in hell is better than living in limbo at the shelter."

He reached out to stroke her cheek. "It must frustrate you to death when they decide to go back. I know you would never have allowed yourself to fall back into a similar situation. You're too strong." His voice stroked her ego as his fingers slid along the curve of her thigh.

She had to remind herself to breathe.

"Yes, it's incredibly frustrating. We get so close to breaking the cycle and then they just waltz back into a situation where they're abused, raped and basically emotionally destroyed by their partner. We nearly get the kids into a world where they won't grow up thinking a screaming match at the dinner table is normal, and then the women go back."

"It's okay. I know you inspire your share of women and those ones don't go back."

She nodded. "Sometimes."

An unobtrusive waiter refilled their champagne glasses. "Are you ready to order?"

Tyler looked at her. "Would you like the lobster?"

"Yes, thank you. You've been incredibly sweet to do all of this for me, especially when I'm the one who got you the shiner." Her eyes were drawn up to the balloons dancing on an unseen draft.

"I got the shiner by sticking my nose into your business—though it allowed me to find out that you are more vital, more real than I ever thought. You excite me," he added for her ears only, and his hand slipped deeper between her legs.

But he nodded at the waiter as if he wasn't making love to her under the table. "We'll both have the lobster."

She tapped her fingers on the table, and then by sheer strength of will stopped them. "How much of the conversation in the kitchen did you overhear?"

"Just enough to make me admire you even more." His fingers teased.

"Stop." She didn't know if she was objecting to the intensity of his touch, or his admiration. "This is simple. Let's not make it complicated."

"Tell me about the foster homes you were in as a child."

She resisted the urge to throw the champagne in his face. There were probably former and future paying clients in this restaurant. "I thought you heard almost nothing."

"That is almost nothing. I'd like you to tell me more. I thought you were amazing before—now I think you're extraordinary."

"Let's talk about sex instead." Her left hand was back in his lap.

The response was subtle, but she was a lawyer: the little blink and the intake of breath satisfied her need for revenge.

"I appreciate the offer."

"Good—" she put his hand on her naked knee "—because I'm looking forward to a little public fondling, and then a hot and heavy session with The Bandit." She held up her glass in a salute, finally feeling back in control of the situation. "How does that sound?"

"It sounds wonderful." His eyes flared in the candlelight.

Without fumbling, his clever fingers found their opening and gently entered her.

She thought she might go up in smoke.

He stroked once, twice and then he pulled his fingers away. "We don't want to rush this."

Bereft of his touch, she sipped champagne and watched as he reached for an oyster in a half shell, which he quickly swallowed. "That was delicious." He licked his lips and captivated her with the heat of his gaze.

Dangerous, challenging, he was every inch her Bandit.

Did he want her as much as she wanted him? She reached over to find out.

"Oh, that's good," she purred, leaning in close. "So good. Is it good for you?" It was if the tight fit of his pants was any indication.

Did he swallow hard?

She took her hand away. She had to keep in mind they were in a restaurant. She needed to figure out how to please him without going overboard.

"Do you want a piece of crab cake?" he asked thickly.

"Yes, please."

He held up the fork, and then he watched her avidly as she sucked the treat into her mouth.

"I love watching you. You're so beautiful. And I don't just mean your features and your perfect figure. I mean, the way you move. It's smooth, graceful and..."

"Seductive?" They had to stay away from the mushy stuff. Surely he knew what she wanted from him. She'd been telling him for months. But why did it suddenly feel as if there was a possibility for more? Just a hint of something she'd never felt before?

He held out another bite. She took it carefully from the fork, but it seemed to stick in her throat. She nodded, and then grabbed her water. The soothing liquid washed away the lump.

It was this restaurant, his chivalry and Emma's in- fluence. *You'll wake up tomorrow and realize his breath is gross, he snorts in his sleep and you won't be able to get out of his place fast enough.*

Tyler offered her another bite of crab cake and it went down easier.

"The food is delicious," she told him.

"I'll bet it's not the only thing that's delicious. I can't wait to have you all to myself. You'll certainly taste better than anything else."

"What a sensual thing to say." She put her finger on the top of the butter, smearing it on, and then licked it off, thoroughly, suggestively. "I know you'll taste really good, too."

"Hmm." He seemed mesmerized. His fork hung in the air.

"The crab cake is getting cold."

"They can heat it up," he said absently, still looking at her like she was the morsel he wanted to scoop up.

Enough of this. She was dying for his touch. She took the hand that had been sitting on the inside of her thigh and moved it directly between her legs. "Now you're getting to the *heat* of the matter."

"Oh, yeah." It sounded like a prayer. Those naughty fingers slid past the garter to pet her. "Watch out, or The Bandit will steal your heart."

It felt so good, every teasing stroke. She was so hungry for him. "I don't think I have a heart to steal, but I won't mind being ravaged."

One of his fingers slid inside of her.

She sighed as he moved it in and out and then rubbed it in exactly the right spot on her clit. His touch stole her breath away.

"Is this what you want?" He pointed at the wine menu. But his fingers dipped deeper.

"Yes." She leaned into his touch, barely able to draw a breath.

"But if I do this, and this, then how will you eat your lobster?"

The little wriggle of his fingers almost got her off.

She scooted back, where he couldn't reach her as deeply and where she could almost think. But his touch still grazed her, sending shivers through her.

Longing to touch him in return, she didn't actually dare. Afraid the intensity of her response would surely show up on her face. Still, she could touch him verbally. "I'll suck it, and nibble it, and then I'll swallow everything."

He moved closer, his touch going deeper. She felt her eyes glazing over at the pleasure of it.

Then the waiter came out of nowhere to bring two steaming plates to the table. The lobsters were huge, beautiful and set in a bed of salad, loose crab meat and tiny shrimps.

But Tina wanted to cry when Tyler withdrew his hand from her lap in order to accept the silver tools they would use to crack the lobster. His hand actually trembled and for a second she thought he'd drop the utensils. That gave her some satisfaction.

"Is there anything else I can get for you?" the waiter asked.

Both of them shook their heads, and murmured their thanks.

Tina could hardly think about anything except that the waiter was walking away, which meant those fingers could resume their dance across her flesh. She felt so bereft without his hand between her legs. It was unusual for her to want a man so badly, but it was surely because of his amazing technique and The Bandit fantasy.

She had another fantasy: Tyler picking her up in his arms and then laying her down like a centerpiece in the middle of the snowy-white tablecloth. The entire restaurant watched as he pulled her dress up, baring her skin. Then he unbuttoned her blouse, loosening the mounds of her breasts. In her mind, she was naked on the table in the midst of the lobster feast, with Tyler running his hands over her. Worshiping her.

"Tina are you there? Do you need something?" Tyler waved the cracking utensil under her nose.

"I'm totally with you," she whispered.

She was with him in her daydream. He grabbed the little pitcher of warm, melted butter and drizzled it over her breasts. Nipples hardening from the heat, she was utterly aroused. He sucked the rich liquid, drop by drop off her nipples. His buttery fingers slid over her lips, down her throat, plucked her nipples and then slid down the hill of her belly button to her hips.

Then he paused, looking down on her almost reverently, seducing her with that scoundrel smile.

"Is there something wrong with your lobster?" Tyler sounded confused and possibly a little hurt.

"No." Absently, she took a bite of the bread she'd buttered earlier.

She shivered, vividly imagining what would come next.

Raising the little butter pitcher as if in a toast, he

dripped it directly between her thighs. The heat made her lift her hips off the table, bringing her to the right height for Tyler to suck the butter off her clit. He dipped inside of her with his tongue and she was lost....

Tina shifted.

The vision was so arousing.

Tyler definitely had that reverence thing going. He always handled her like she was the most precious woman he'd ever touched.

And he'd brought her balloons.

She shook her head. Somehow dwelling on the sexual fantasy was safer than thinking about the significance of the balloons.

She barely resisted the urge to stroke herself under the tablecloth. She picked up a little fork and pulled the flesh from the middle of the lobster, where they'd broken it open. It tasted like urgent, sizzling sex. Adding the butter sauce actually caused a trickle of moisture between her legs.

"How is your lobster?" she asked with husky innocence, tearing off another piece of the succulent flesh.

"Tina, I can't eat I want you so badly."

She brushed her aching nipple subtly with the inside of her arm. "How do you know I want *you?*"

"Because you've got that look. Your eyes are as golden as the butter. When I put my fingers inside of you I want you to suck on this lobster."

"I'll pretend I'm sucking on you."

"Oh."

He leaned in to touch her face as he ran his finger

along her thigh. Unerringly he found the heat of her, and she sucked a fat piece of lobster into her mouth. She could feel the thick wetness between her legs and pretended Tyler was there with the butter and his thick cock.

"You're making love to that lobster," he whispered.

"I wish I had you on the table with the butter."

He made a sound like a groan and he put more pressure inside of her. She tried to concentrate on the lobster but she was on the verge.

"I'm going to ravage you. I'm going to take you so many times tonight that you're going to be totally sated."

Thrusting, stopping, he drove her almost to the edge.

"I want you, too." She panted. "I want you to take me all the way."

"You want me?" He gave up all pretense of eating and leaned close enough to penetrate her more deeply.

She almost dropped her cracker. "More," she breathed.

"Anything for you." He thrust.

Tina felt the wave come over her and she clung to his hand under the table. She didn't make a sound but she couldn't hear or see for a few seconds. "Oh."

He removed his hand and righted the skirt of her dress. "Are you feeling all right?" he asked like the naughty satyr of midsummer, come to life. The restaurant had never looked more magical. Was that why she'd never felt like this before? She was caught up in the magical backdrop?

"Hmmm, I'm actually feeling wonderful." She made direct eye contact. "Thank you."

"It was my pleasure, too."

That made her giggle. He sure knew how to take care of her. Maybe she should keep him around longer. "I like this romantic stuff. I guess I'm a sap like Emma after all."

"Maybe it's *me* you like."

She opened her mouth to refute what he'd said. But all evidence pointed to it being Tyler who kindled the magic. Tyler who wanted a little more out of the relationship and had actually earned it. Could she take this further than she'd taken any other liaison? Could she love more than his sexual technique? Like his naughty grin and his tenderness? This man who gave her balloons *and* mind-blowing orgasms?

Had she fallen for him? Over lobster? Did it get any better than she had it right now? She couldn't imagine.

"Sweetheart?"

This time the endearment didn't sound as strange. She thought she might be able to get used to being called pet names. "What?" she said absently.

"Are you okay?"

"I'm wonderful. I'm not sure I could stand at the moment but I'm great. Just great."

"Just wait till we have some privacy." His smile was all male arrogance, and for once she didn't mind.

"Why?" she whispered. "Will you strip me naked and lay me on a table like a feast?" She sucked the end of the lobster claw. "Will you dip me in butter and slide your fingers and your cock inside of me until I come?"

He didn't speak for a moment, then said, "I thought we agreed this kind of behavior could get us into trouble." His grin told her that he didn't really give a damn.

"I'm already in trouble." It was heartfelt.

He put his hand on her leg.

She slid it immediately to where she needed him. Again.

"You are so ready for me." He sighed in her ear, nuzzling her neck. "I wish I could dip my lobster here, it would taste so good."

She barely breathed. Aching. Needing like never before. Vulnerable like never before.

He held her securely by the shoulder, pretending to be leaning against her. With one hidden hand buried in her silky flesh, he gave her more. She barely wondered if her face was giving her away, what people might think. There was only the need to feel....

Those fingers penetrated her deeper. She put her head down, clenching the tablecloth. He pushed farther. She whimpered. Deeper. Biting her lip she felt the need give way to a tearing, breaking orgasm that left her limp upon the table.

Never had she given anyone this power over her, she thought as she came back to herself. But maybe this time not everything came back. Maybe this time a little bit of Tina had been given into Tyler's keeping. What would he do with that part of her? How could she trust this?

She heard Tyler speaking to the waiter. Eventually she was able to raise her head up off the table and push the hair off her sweaty face.

"You've been crying," Tyler muttered at her. "They're bringing the check. You lost a client—

suicide—and it's been eating you all day. I tried to cheer you up because it's your birthday but all I've done is upset you."

She blinked. "Counselor, you can tell a tall tale."

"I've had practice. I'm a lawyer."

She smirked, then took a cleansing breath.

"This way you get lots of sympathy, we don't get disbarred and I only look like an insensitive jerk for giving you balloons on such a horrible day."

"Thanks for covering my ass. And everything else."

"Oh, honey, I'm going to cover it. I'm going to touch you everywhere as soon as I get you to bed. In fact, the only reason we're taking the lobster to go is so that I can hide my huge hard-on behind a really big bag. I've been trying to put out the fire long enough to get you out of here but I'm afraid there's only one solution."

"Let's go to my place." Where had that come from?

"I'd love to but I've got to take care of the dogs first."

"Okay, then we'll stay at your place. I don't think I can wait to have your cock deep inside of me."

"Yes."

"Yes to what?"

"Yes to everything." He laughed hoarsely. "I want you so much I'm going to explode with it. I can't believe we came in two cars."

She giggled half-hysterically at the thought of making love in her little car.

The waiter with the doggie bag came with an appropriately sympathetic aura. Tina tried to look like a woman who'd just burst into tears in public, though she'd never done such a foolish thing in her life. "I want the balloons," she blurted out.

Both Tyler and the waiter looked at her in surprise.

She tried to look subdued. "Well, he went to so much trouble, and I feel so bad for breaking down like this…." She actually found it in her to sniff a little bit.

The men scrambled for the balloons as if they feared another outburst of tears. She kept her head bowed, lest they see the mirth in her eyes. In minutes, she and Tyler were walking out of Lagoona's. Out on the sidewalk she started laughing.

"What are you laughing about?" he cried. "I barely got us out of there with our professional reputations intact. You're one wild woman." The bag hung strategically in front of him. The balloons bobbed above them.

"Hey, you weren't exactly an angel in there."

"Do you always behave this badly in public?"

That sobered her. "Never."

"Do you want to do it again soon?" The naughty look was back in his eyes.

"Oh, yes." She didn't dare kiss him again, but she wanted to. What a strange, heady sensation.

"Meet me at my house? Promise? I'll take these balloons so you don't have to try to see around them. And that way I know you'll come to my place to get them because you asked for them."

She leaned into him and gave him a passionate, hungry kiss. "I plan to get a very expensive speeding ticket getting to your house."

Sliding into her car, she met his eyes for a moment.

Then she had to look down in order to concentrate on getting the car started. When she looked up he was gone. Did her heart sink? She'd heard that expression but never thought to experience it in a relationship situation.

She pointed the car in the direction of his house, knowing she drove a perilous road, one she had no experience with, one she'd never thought to travel.

Still, recklessly, she raced forward.

8

THE HEAVYSET, unkempt man yelled. Tina hadn't done the chores the way he wanted. Of course, the mower was huge compared to the little girl, which didn't seem to bother him. She tried to tell him how hard she'd worked. Her arms ached from maneuvering the heavy machine around the yard. His wife came out of the house to start a yelling match right there in front of the neighbors.

Tina cringed.

"I told you to get a boy. Why can't we ever get a boy so I can get some help around here? If you'd mow the yard once in a while, your ass wouldn't be as big as the chair."

"My ass? What about the belly hanging in front of you? You think I find it attractive? You're disgusting. And if you don't leave the babysitter alone, I'm going to tell her parents."

Then Tyler was there, holding a take-out bag in front of him. "It hides a multitude of sins," he told her smugly.

"What if we end up like them?" Tina gestured toward the couple on the lawn.

He glanced over dismissively. "We're not them. We're just having sex."

"Yes." She breathed. "That's easier."

Emma appeared beside her. "You have to admit you have feelings for him."

"I don't work that way!" Tina protested. She looked down. She looked like the frog in the restaurant. An ugly brown frog. "I'm a frog."

"A frog princess. Tyler will save you," the wise Emma told her.

"I can save myself," Tina protested. "Remember how hard you worked to learn to be independent, and then you just gave it all up to Tony?"

"But whom did I give myself, too? That's the important question. You have to pick the right person."

A whole line of animals—a tiger, snake, ape and more—milled around, each of them with a face from her past.

Tyler pushed through the parade of animals. "You can trust me."

They all started yelling, growling, chirping, hissing and meowing, until Tina had to cover her ears. "I have to think," she said. "I have to think."

It seemed to echo until it faded to a gentle snoring sound....

Tyler, the perfect man, was emitting soft snoring sounds. His long body wrapped around her like the snake from her dream. Tina struggled against his hold until he rolled over in the opposite direction.

Suddenly she couldn't hear the snoring, she couldn't

feel him and, fighting a wave of anxiety, she scooted back until her leg touched his. Then, with the sounds of the animals from her dreams threading through her mind like a bad song, she drifted back to sleep, exhausted from making love to Tyler well into the dawn.

"HEY, TINA, you're hogging the bed."

His voice sounded so sexy in the morning.

"And you snore," she muttered, not to be outdone.

He slid his arms around her waist. "What do you want to do today? The zoo? A water park? We can go to the arcade."

"What?" she asked groggily. "Is this your usual lineup for dates? Or is there something about me that brings out the kid in you?"

"You bring *up* all sorts of things in me."

She could feel his morning erection pressing against her butt. "Not yet, tiger. I'm not into sex before coffee."

I usually never spend the night with the guy. That's probably why I had that silly nightmare.

To tell the truth, it didn't feel so bad to be with Tyler this morning, snoring and all. It felt kind of cozy.

"So what do you want to do today?" he asked again.

"Do you have to have an itinerary right this minute?" she grumped at him.

"You don't like mornings." He sounded pleased.

"Who does? Especially after you kept me up half of the night."

He ran his hands over the curve of her ass. "I couldn't resist you."

She pushed his hands away. Even if he could rouse her this morning, it was the principal of the thing. "Coffee."

"Okay," he said agreeably. "I'll bring you some coffee while you think of what you want to do today. Do we have to go by your place? Get some clothes? Water the plants? Feed the cat?"

"Very funny. Are you making fun of me because I'm not a slave to a pet or a plant? I swear I'm going to get a feline and pray that you're actually allergic."

"Hmm. I'll have to bribe you not to do it. Somebody we both know and love doesn't like cats in a big way."

She caught the gleam in his eyes, and she automatically put her hands up. "Don't bring Frosty in here. I'm not into a face wash before I have my coffee, and if you have any hopes of putting that morning erection to good use, you'd better be nice."

He jumped out of bed. "I'm nice. I promise, I'm very nice."

After the coffee, she found him very nice indeed.

"I DON'T KNOW WHY you're being so stubborn about this. It's just one more night. And you don't have anything needing attention back at your place." He reached down to scratch the dog as if to taunt her that he did have things at home needing attention.

Who cared if he had a couple of dumb dogs? Did it make him mentally healthier, or just dumber? Since they'd spent a good part of the day walking and bathing the dogs, it obviously made him a slave to the critters.

Although it had been kind of fun.

"I just need some space. Understand?" She hated sounding like she was apologizing. "I'm feeling restless. I'm having weird dreams and I just want to go home." She'd had another one of those crazy dreams after they'd taken a long afternoon nap to make up for their nighttime, morning and afternoon activities.

Tina looked at his video selection. Which one of these movies would make a good cry movie? And why did she feel the need to cry? Why did Emma have to be out of town when she needed her? When had she allowed herself to need Emma anyway? And more importantly, what would she do if she allowed herself to need Tyler?

She pushed back her hair. "I'm falling apart. I really have to go home."

"Can I come with you?"

"No, I need to be alone."

"I know what that means." He lowered his head.

She'd never been the crying type. It seemed to solve nothing at all, just complicated everything. Yet today, after a wonderful day, she seemed to have an ocean of tears lodged in her throat. Because being with him felt right. Because it felt better than right.

She needed to get out of here because being totally vulnerable to him wasn't in the plan. Not now. Not ever.

And he had only to put his talented hands on her in order to convince her to stay. It was part of his plan. He'd even had the gall to admit it. When had it all gotten so complicated?

"Come and sit with me on the couch just for a few minutes before you take off. Please?"

"I don't think so."

"I was hoping you'd get accustomed to being here, with us. I thought it might be fun to see how it goes."

"How it goes?" she repeated dumbly. Was this more of his plan? "It goes like we have sex, and then I go *home*."

"What's wrong? We've had a great day."

She licked her lips. "It's been a nice, relaxing day, and now I go home and prepare for my work week. Thank you for having me."

"Thank you for having me? So formal. Like we haven't been naked nearly all weekend."

She threw up her hands. "What do you want me to say? No thank you? It was awesome, but…?"

"Say you'll come back and stay with me next weekend."

She shrugged. "I'm sure I have plans."

Tyler patted the couch next to him. "Sit with me for just a few minutes. Don't be afraid."

Her head came up. "I'm not afraid. Don't treat me like a child."

Tyler wanted to soothe her the way he would Frosty, but she'd gone all prickly on him. They were both novices in the relationship game. She'd apparently never gotten close enough and he'd always gotten bored before it could be considered a relationship.

Not having a clue wasn't going to stop him, though. Patting the seat beside him, he wished he had some sort of treat to bring her to him as easily as he enticed Frosty. All he had right now to lure her to him was patience and persistence.

With reluctance, she came and sat on the couch. For a few minutes she was tense, but then Frosty jumped up on the cushions and lay on her legs.

"See, it's not so hard."

"Stop teasing, or I'll just go."

As she stroked the pup's soft ears, he held her, enjoying the rare moment when the restless energy driving her had ebbed away.

One hand crept up the back of her neck to cup the back of her head and stroke the silken cap of her hair. He held her tenderly, showing her everything he felt for her, all the love she wouldn't accept.

As if she sensed his unspoken emotions, she tensed up in his arms.

Then a tear landed inside of his elbow. Why was she crying? "Do you have something in your contact?"

"No." There was a delicate sniffle. "I don't wear contacts."

"Are you injured?"

"No. Yes."

He paused, momentarily speechless.

Another tear dripped on his arm.

Panic started to set in and in his lawyer's voice he inquired, "May we back up to the preceding question? Are you injured? Is the answer no or yes?"

"The witness should answer the question." It might have been an attempt at a joke, but she sounded as if she were choking as she wrenched herself out of his arms.

He didn't try to hold her. He'd learned enough about her to realize he couldn't hang on to her against her will. He had to make *her* want *him*—emotionally, since they had the physical stuff down.

She hunched away from him. "You hurt me by being so damn persistent. I keep telling you that I don't want this. I can't afford this emotional crap. I won't go through all of this again."

"Why is the emotional stuff called *crap?*"

"Because it is. Stuff doesn't last, so why get into a big fuss?"

"You mean relationships don't last."

"Yeah."

"But half of all marriages last a lifetime."

She curled in on herself. "You sound just like someone I know. How can you be so stupid? Have you ever looked inside those marriages that last? Those people are having affairs with the babysitter or a neighbor, beating their children, spending money they don't have or simply stagnating. If you look, you'll see the dysfunction. There's no such thing as a good marriage, just a bunch of saps too weak to let go of a dead relationship."

"While you haven't seen the positive side of marriage, at least you're aware of all the pitfalls. That insight could keep us out of trouble."

Her head came up.

"Hypothetically speaking," he said hurriedly.

Hadn't he just decided he wouldn't force it for fear she'd sprint out of his life?

"I can't seem to see beyond my fears."

"You could let me guide you into a relationship, regardless of your innate fears. After all, my parents have had a good relationship for thirty-five years so I'm practically an expert." He had to bite his lip to keep from laughing.

She pulled away from him. "No way am I going to...oh, you're kidding, right?"

He picked up her hand and then kissed it. "Yes, I'm kidding." Tina wasn't meant to be humbled. He had no intention of humbling her, ever. He loved everything about her, especially her fierce spirit. "We would sit and talk if we had a problem. We're two smart, respectful people. We would try to come up with a solution if something seemed to be going wrong."

"I grew up in a series of foster homes. Six to be exact. How would I know what to do with a relationship, even if we talk it out? I might yell first, and then talk later."

He sucked in a breath. It hit him pretty hard every time he realized how far he'd been off in his assumptions of her background. Before he'd learned a bit about her, he'd imagined she came from old money, east coast, with servants and polo horses. He'd thought she'd probably skipped her debutante ball to go out drinking with the guys, but never once had he considered the possibility she was an orphan.

"You might yell. That's okay. I might yell, too. But

we're both accustomed to controlling our emotions in the courtroom. We can do it in the relationship, just enough not to trample the other person's feelings when we say what we think and feel."

"You've been thinking about this," she accused him.

"Yes, I have." He held his breath.

"I can't think about it. I can't possibly get it right and it makes me feel sad. I don't cry. I don't cry."

But she looked ready to cry. "Tina, don't fight it. Do what feels right. You can grow into it like you did with Emma." He pulled her against him and held her there until she relaxed just the tiniest bit. "Doesn't this feel good? We could be so good together."

"I just can't. I'm no Emma. Maybe she and Tony have a chance, but I never would." She shook her head. "Emma calls every couple of days from the islands to tell me about her marital bliss, and it's driving me crazy. It's probably responsible for my crazy dreams. And my crazier ideas."

"What ideas?" For a minute he felt almost hopeful.

"Nothing."

He waited.

She fidgeted with her fingers, then stopped. "It's just this together stuff. It makes me want things that are not realistic. I have to fight it. I have to *go*." She pulled away from him.

"I won't hurt you," he promised, knowing she wouldn't understand the commitment behind his words.

She made a wiping motion at her beautiful eyes, and his heart contracted. He couldn't bear for her to cry. He never would have guessed the toughest bitch lawyer in town had it in her to cry. "Please, won't you let me hold you? Comfort you? I wouldn't mind." Wasn't that the understatement of the year? He longed to wrap his arms around her forever and kiss those tears away.

"If you touch me right now, I'll scratch your eyes out," she said with more bravado than she appeared to be feeling. "The only thing holding me back is the cost of this manicure. I don't want to mess it up."

"Okay. I guess I'm lucky your manicure's so expensive. See how well we communicate?"

Another sort of choking laugh, but then she buried her head in the pillow with a fresh sob.

He squirmed. He'd faced many tears in his time as a lawyer, so why did hers freak him out? "I could tell you some of my niece's cannibal jokes. That might cheer you up. Like why did the cannibal husband complain to the cannibal wife? Because she gave him the *cold* shoulder."

"Oh, God," she practically whimpered.

"Hey, the joke's not that bad." He inched back toward her on the couch.

She held up her hand as if to fend him off. "Go away. I don't cry. I don't fall apart. You never saw this. Understand?"

The tough act would have been much more convincing without the fresh wave of tears and the wobbling voice. "You want me to go away and give you some privacy? I guess I could take the dogs on another walk."

"Yes. Please."

She sounded like he was giving her a gift. By leaving. It was pitiful.

He took a huge leap. Probably off a cliff. "Is this privacy for tonight or forever? If you leave, are you going to come back?"

Another sniff.

The silence lengthened.

Buttoning his shirt, Tyler barely breathed, wondering if and how she'd answer his question. But Tina only pulled an afghan over her. Tyler slipped out the door without a confrontation, without asking any more questions, and without touching her as he ached to do. The only comfort he could give her at the moment was the comfort of solitude.

After a long, painful walk he came home, and found her gone. *He* found no comfort in the solitude. None at all.

Frosty immediately jumped on the couch when Tyler sat down. Absently he stroked the pup. "She's gone, boy."

Frosty yawned.

"I'm going to have to back off and give her a little time, even if I just want to show up at her door and carry her away in The Bandit costume."

The dog yawned again.

"Yeah, great. You're full of good advice. I could be like you and show her shameless attention, however many times she throws it back in my face, but I'm just not that patient."

Frosty whined.

"Okay, I guess I can be somewhat patient."

Except I always lose my head, when I touch her, when sex is involved, when I look at how hot she is, when I want her, which is damn near all of the time. I'm not used to having that particular complication.

He could walk away. Take on a less complicated case. Exactly how badly did he want her?

Pretty badly.

"I'm afraid I'm a goner, boy. Down for the count. Hung jury." *Hell, I actually told her a cannibal joke and even offered to take her to a water park. Of course, she'd look spectacular in a bathing suit.*

Scratching Frosty's ears until the pup went into an ecstasy of leg thumping, Tyler told the dog, "I just didn't expect her to cry. Maybe it's progress. Or maybe she'll never speak to me again."

He let the pup take a breather as he brushed the white dog hair off the couch. *If sex is really all she wants from me, could I accept a relationship like that? Of course not.*

Then Tyler grinned. *Who am I kidding? I couldn't forgo sex.* "All she would have to do is start taking off her clothes. With her, I have the self-control of a dog. No offense, boy."

The dog jumped off the couch. Tyler could hear him nosing around in the bowl in the kitchen. The dog always hoped the bowl would be magically filled. Hope. With Tina's unexpected show of vulnerability, Tyler could allow himself a little hope, as well. His heart felt battered but not shattered. The context had been all wrong; she hadn't even known he was trying to make her a promise. She just wasn't ready. There was a lot for her to get used to.

Patience. The plan for the moment was to be patient and persistent. But he wasn't usually a patient man. It was one of his biggest faults. Boredom had been a lifelong enemy, until he'd met his match. He had no doubts Tina would give him all the challenge he'd ever need, and someday the love, too.

This time it would stick. He would stick.

And he'd make all of his closing arguments irrefutable. He wasn't a top-notch lawyer for nothing.

9

"SO HOW DID Tyler find out about Hideaway House?" Emma asked. It seemed almost unreal to be back in the break room at work after being in heaven on her honeymoon. She grimaced at the way her Jimmy Choo shoes pinched her feet, though they looked good with her tan.

"We're supposed to be talking about your honeymoon, not my problems with Tyler. What happened? Did the stars fall out of the heavens and the clouds float around you the entire time you cruised?" Tina sounded like her old self, but she looked tense.

"Yes!" Emma couldn't help smiling. Her face had been frozen in the position since she'd gotten engaged. Life was wonderful, and she wanted wonderful for her friend Tina. She knew how much pain and loneliness Tina held inside her tough exterior. "It's amazing how liberating it feels to belong to someone, body and soul."

Tina didn't say anything. Emma pictured her biting her tongue to keep her cynical comments to herself.

"Was the honeymoon suite on the ship as incredible as the advertisements we looked at?"

"It was nice, but even nicer on St. Thomas when we

reached the hotel honeymoon suite. We had a private hot tub, fresh flowers and fruit every day, and our own slice of beach with a privacy fence."

"Sand is highly overrated as a place to make out."

Grinning, Emma just nodded.

"Tyler and I did the ocean thing here on the beach. It was pretty great."

Emma felt that silly blush coming on again. "You made love in the ocean? Don't you know there are all kinds of dangerous things swimming around after dark? Things with major teeth."

Tina shrugged. "We did it in daylight. Discreetly, of course."

"Yeah. Discreetly. Are you crazy? After all of your hard work you want to be reported for public indecency?"

"Oh, he's decent. He's incredibly decent."

Emma choked out a laugh. "You're taking too many chances on this one, counselor."

"I know. Absolutely, I know it."

Emma evaluated her friend. "What else did you do?"

Tina looked pensive. "He took me out to Lagoona's and bought me these silly helium balloons. It was kinda childish, but nice. I really expected something more sophisticated from him. I guess I don't know him as well as I thought."

"Did you like the balloons?" Emma didn't know what to think of The Shark being into balloons.

"They get in the way. They keep drifting around the condo, and now they're at waist level."

"You took the balloons home?"

"I couldn't leave them. He went to a lot of trouble."

"Did he get what he wanted?"

"What do you mean?"

"Did you take him home, and make love with him?"

"First, he brought me to a climax twice *in* the restaurant. Then we brought the lobster to his place and did the butter thing on the counter. It was probably the craziest night I've ever had."

Was Tina blushing? Emma couldn't believe it. In the week she'd been on her honeymoon, Tyler had made quite an impression on Tina.

Emma fanned her face with her hand. Wow. Better not to ask for any more detail about the restaurant date, although take-out lobster with butter sauce might make an interesting weekend activity. It would be fascinating, the sucking, the cracking, the sucking…

"Emma?"

"What? Oh, I asked you how he found out about Hideaway House."

"Okay, my legal aide told him. I guess he's been charming her behind my back or something."

"You should fire her. It's not good for her to be giving out personal information."

"It's not her fault he's so smooth. He could convince any woman to do anything." Tina pushed her hair out of her face, obviously frustrated and confused. "He's scary. He set Sam up with this biker, who also happens to be a fairly talented artist with a small trust fund. I checked him out. He's a sort of a knight in biker armor. He's always helping out the homeless, does a lot of charity stuff. So now she sings in Hawaiian when she's cleaning the kitchen. How can I complain when he's making people happy?"

"Is he making you happy?"

"In bed? Sure." Her fingers fidgeted.

"Is he trying to convince you to have a relationship?"

"Of course not. I'm just enjoying his prowess in bed. It's strictly a short-term thing. A relationship has rules and stuff. In a relationship, you have his toothbrush in your bathroom and a spare set of his clothes in your drawer. Or you have all of your stuff at his house where his dogs sit in your lap. You have to talk, but not yell." Tina shook her head as though to clear it and took a deep breath. "I'm not into all of that. All I have is a few silly balloons bouncing around."

"You protest too much."

"And you're such an optimist." Tina reached over to give Emma a spontaneous hug. "And I missed you, tons."

Emma watched, flabbergasted, as Tina rushed from the break room. Her friend had come a long way from the day they'd decided they would go on the singles' cruise. Back when Tina wouldn't have felt comfortable giving a hug. Maybe she was on her way to getting used to other things, too, such as a relationship with Tyler.

Looking down at her wedding rings, Emma giggled. She'd also come a long, long way.

TINA SIGHED. Then she rubbed her fingers together. Yeah, it was an annoying nervous habit, but it was one she could hide beneath the table.

The judge even looked bored. Everyone knew the other lawyer was questioning this witness so he could get grounds for another continuance. Mackee liked to work on his cases as he went along. Tina would swear on the bailiff's bible they hadn't had a case where Mackee didn't come to a screeching halt in the middle of the trial. Maybe he figured it scattered the concentration of the opposing counsel.

It wouldn't matter in the long run. She had the case sewn up tight, despite scattered concentration. Tyler. Tyler was more of a threat to her life, and her career, than anything Mackee might drag out of his newest witness.

"Your Honor, the defense asks for a continuation in this case."

The judge managed not to sigh as he granted the request and gave the defense three days to do whatever grand gesture Mackee had in mind. He was actually a decent lawyer who won more than his share of cases. But not this time. Tina had located several eyewitnesses who were reputable volunteers for the food kitchen, and who happened to be downtown when the beating had occurred. They included a young lawyer and the daughter of a city councilman.

Tina's man, Barkley, wasn't responsible for beating a homeless man practically to death. He'd just been in the wrong place at the wrong time. Being a rich man with a bad attitude, a temper and a cocaine habit didn't make you any friends. The police had enjoyed booking the guy.

Tina rose to her feet as the judge left the courtroom. She nodded at her legal assistant, then consulted with her client. Barkley had a surly attitude since cocaine was hard to come by in jail. Also, with his record with law enforcement, the bail had been set high. It took her a few minutes to put him in his place before she sent him off with the bailiff.

On her way down the hall, a man in cuffs screamed obscenities at the press. People grieved. Others smiled to have received justice, or the nearest thing to it.

Life as a lawyer was never dull.

She gripped her leather briefcase tighter. This was the only place she felt at home. Here she fought the battles she'd been denied as a child. Most of her cases included fat fees, as well as justice, but she balanced it out by giving time to the women and children at Hideaway House.

Tyler understood this part of her life. In the beginning she'd dated other lawyers. But in time, she'd discovered that lawyers who were successful had big egos, and any man with an ego couldn't take his lady being more successful than he was. She had a long way to go to be as successful as Tyler. He'd already made partner in a very prestigious firm.

He hadn't called Monday or Tuesday and for some reason it had grinded on her. Balloons had been delivered on Wednesday, so she'd been able to breathe again, though her dependency caused her anxiety. Then he'd made a very casual call on Thursday, and tonight they had a date at an arcade, of all places. Tina shook her head. Why the man wanted to do kid stuff was beyond her.

A few hours later, she pulled in at the arcade for adults, still feeling a bit bemused. Tyler met her just inside the door. He shifted from foot to foot as if full of energy.

"Hey. I'm here," she told him without enthusiasm.

He swept her up in a huge hug. "I missed you. You look beautiful."

She opened her mouth, but she couldn't actually admit she'd missed him.

Intimately, he whispered in her ear, "And I missed your body."

"We could skip the arcade and find a place," she offered. She'd missed his body, too. Desperately.

"No, I can wait until you lose everything to me first. Then I'll cash in my chips, so to speak." He rubbed his hands together. "Prepare to be womped on."

"Right." The challenge had her blood singing. His hand on her arm and the delicious scent of his cologne had an even greater effect. What the man did to a pair of jeans and a black T-shirt should have been illegal.

As they made their way into the building, she found the arcade an eyeful. High tech. There was even a bar. She'd never really seen anything like it on this scale. She'd certainly never had the money in college to spend on this kind of frivolous entertainment. She'd had to fight for every dollar, be it grant or scholarship, and had gone without to make ends meet.

Hence the lavish restaurants and the expensive clothing she now enjoyed. It wasn't just part of her lawyer uniform; it was also a type of reassurance. She'd beaten the system she'd been told couldn't be beaten.

"What do you want to do first?" He rubbed his hands together.

She shrugged. "I have no idea. Show me everything."

"Shall we race cars or spaceships? Do you want to do motocross or skiing? It's all here and it's pretty realistic."

She began to feel a sense of excitement. "Where do we start?"

They loaded their plastic cards with credits, and then headed over to the cars. They were the shells of race cars complete with steering wheels. She climbed in and studied the screen, trying to absorb enough information to be competitive.

"Are you ready to go? Or are you afraid I'll beat the pants off of you?"

"Just try it." She practiced with the steering wheel to get a feel for it. Then she played with the gear shift thing on the floor. "Maybe I'll be the one taking down your pants."

"What?"

"You know, slowly lowering them to the floor while I fondle you."

"Are you serious?"

He appeared to be drooling a little.

"Any suggestions?" she asked.

"We could leave right now."

"I mean, with this game."

"What?"

"Are you always this easy to distract? How do you ever win a case when there's a sexy woman involved?"

"Most women don't look like you, and they don't cheat like you."

"I'm not cheating. I'd be happy to follow through."

"Really?" He looked so hopeful.

She shrugged. "I might feel like it. Later. If I win. I'm a poor loser so I probably won't feel like having sex if I lose."

"You're definitely not a good sport, are you?"

"But I'm a hell of a lay."

He looked really torn. "Okay."

"Okay, what? You can't throw all the races and games. It'll take the fun out of it."

His smile had serious wattage behind it. "You make it difficult, but I'll try to honor your request."

"Good. Now tell me how to win this race."

"Keep to the inside lane, and expect to be blown away, sweetheart."

"You think you're such a hot *rod,*" she said, shaking her head at her own bad joke.

His grin was instantaneous and combustive.

She pushed the button to start. "Which destination should I choose?" she asked as she studied the choices.

"I'll take you to paradise by the dashboard lights."

Trite as the reference was, it gave her goose bumps; they hadn't made it in a car. Yet. "That isn't one of the destinations on the screen," she reprimanded him.

"Okay, later then." With expertise she envied, he punched in the necessary information, and they were off. She enjoyed everything, the great graphics, the funny road obstacles, even the police chasing her as she went through a city block. Of course, Tyler beat her because she kept running into the side of the road. The steering was hard to get used to, and it overcorrected.

"Yup, I'm the man," he crowed.

"We'll see," she muttered. "I didn't come close to winning, and it's winning that turns me on." Usually. Apparently, it didn't take more than his little-boy grin to turn her on right at this moment.

"What did you say? You're turned on?" He leaned in close enough to kiss her.

She jerked back. "Nothing important. Just swipe your card, and let's race again. I intend to do better this time around."

"You can never do better than me. Why don't you just relax and enjoy the ride?" He patted her arm.

She made eye contact. "I'll ride *you* today, but tomorrow I'm trading up."

He narrowed his gaze. "Are you willing to up the ante?"

"What? Ten dollars a race? Twenty?" She ran her nails over the soft cotton of his shirt. Her touch had his male nipples standing up like little soldiers. She thought about the destination choices that had been on the screen. "I want to go to the Indy 500 this time."

"You can't handle the 500." His tone was almost painful since she had him by the collar, literally. "You're just a beginner."

She leaned in until she could smell his cologne. "I wish we were alone so I could ride in your lap, naked, while we play."

His Adam's apple bobbed. "Sounds good. I'll buy one of these things on eBay. Tomorrow."

She reached up to kiss him playfully on the cheek. "You're too easy."

"Only for you."

That shook her. He sounded as if he really meant it. "Are we gonna play, or what?"

"Oh, yeah."

She pulled away, disgruntled. Everything they said and did had that sexual edge of new lovers, but they'd been together long enough it should have worn off. Why hadn't it worn off?

"Just shut up, and set up the 500." She climbed into the car impatiently. "What's wrong?" she asked. "Why aren't we going already?"

"We haven't settled on the stakes."

"What do you want?"

"A foot rub."

That surprised her. It didn't sound even remotely sensual. "Yuck. I don't do feet."

"That's why they call it the agony of de-feet." He laughed.

Her heart lurched, not at the silly joke, but at the way he looked stuffed in the car and playing like a little boy. It made her feel young and silly—she hadn't ever felt that way. "Okay. Anything else?"

"We could go for more fantasy. You seemed to like The Bandit."

That sounded dangerous. Better to keep this light. "Why don't we just play for beers?"

Beer was impersonal, and the bar was a good place to look for a man who didn't threaten her sense of security.

"Beers? You drink beer?"

"I was in college twice as long as most people."

"It's just that you're so elegant. Lobster, champagne, those things I can see, but not beer. Do you drink it out of a bottle?"

"Of course."

He pressed the start button for the race and she leaned forward, concentrating.

And damned if he didn't win again. "That just bagged me a foot massage," he crowed as he climbed out of the car. "Now let's go see if you're a skier or a flier."

He watched the way her slim hips rocked as they walked. He loved the way her heels made her sway. Of course, he also loved her barefoot in his home, and especially buck naked in his bed.

They approached a popcorn and cotton candy display. She seemed to study it as they passed so he bought her both popcorn and cotton candy in a revolting shade of pink and yellow, just to watch her smile: "I think you should save some of this. I wouldn't mind licking it off your skin. It melts like sugar." He thought about all the naughty places he could put the sweet stuff.

She grinned with candy-pink lips. "It does. I never knew it just melted in your mouth. I'll never get it all off my fingers," she said, licking her digits.

Biting back a groan, he tried to think about something besides how sexy she was when she let her guard down. He was going to have her until he couldn't move a muscle.

Then he was going to send Sam roses. Bringing out the kid in Tina had helped immeasurably.

He spent the rest of the evening subtly losing so he could watch Tina get excited. She did drink beer, and pigged out on hot wings. The beer seemed to make her affectionate, on the couch, in the kitchen and especially in bed. As Tyler fell into an exhausted sleep, he vowed to stock enough beer to make the Budweiser company very happy.

10

TINA WOKE TO FIND a muscular arm flung across her, pinning her to the bed. She groaned. Not again. She'd also had another unsettling dream. This time she'd been looking for her mother and father. Every time she'd spotted them, they'd just faded away.

She brushed the tears from the corner of her eyes. "It wasn't their fault they died in that car crash," she muttered. "And anyway, I made all of my dreams come true all by myself."

"Are you okay, baby?"

Tyler's guttural voice wrapped around her and she felt more tears threaten. "Of course I'm okay. I don't need you to comfort me." *I don't need anyone. I can handle it. I'm strong enough. No matter what's happened in my life, I've always been strong enough.* But it was becoming a physical effort to hold back the tears.

Lifting his head, he peered at her through slitted eyes. It should have been cute but she was in no mood for cute.

"Comfort you? You hurting? What do ya need?"

"I don't need anything!" She shoved at his arm.

"Move, you're strangling me!" He obligingly moved his arm, and she slid out from under the summer comforter. Then she stomped into the kitchen with enough force to hurt the balls of her feet.

Waiting for the coffeepot seemed to take forever and she felt cold enough to wrap her arms around herself. This was crazy. It wasn't cold and she wasn't upset over a stupid dream.

"I would have made coffee."

"You don't need to wait on me."

He leaned casually on the counter. "What do you want to do today?"

"I should head home."

"We've been over this before."

"I know."

"It's easier to have sex if we're in the same place," he pointed out obligingly. "How about we go and get a few things that you might need from your place before we head to the aquarium? They have the best exhibits, and there's a brand new whale show."

"I never saw the old one," Tina muttered into the coffee she'd poured.

"It's great. I always think I'm in the wrong profession when I see the trainers riding the killer whales. What an ass-kicking job."

Tina could feel her eyes get wider. "They actually ride them?"

"Yeah. Haven't you ever seen it on TV?"

Tina shook her head. "I've seen specials on the killer whale on the nature channel." She tried to check her enthusiasm so she didn't sound silly. "I think it sounds like fun, actually."

"Okay. We'll have to get your suit because it's gonna be hot, and the water park will allow us to cool off."

"Do you think a thong is appropriate?" she teased.

"Only if you want to cause a stampede."

She grinned. "Okay. I'll get something more conservative." He always seemed to want her. It inspired her more than the coffee, so she hurried him back to bed for a quickie.

Sex was easy and, as it turned out, so was Tyler.

LATER INTO THE work week, Tina sat in on the depositions from the incident at the shelter. It was definitely an experience, because the women generally praised Tyler to death.

By noon, Tina was fidgeting. By two, she desperately needed a nail file. Then when they got to Lisa, the woman defended her husband and refused to press charges. Fortunately, she'd previously filed the protective order, so the D.A. didn't need anything further to file charges, especially with all of the testimony from the other women.

But listening to Lisa defend her deadbeat husband made Tina feel tired and angry. Why did she bother to take on these cases when the women so often insisted on going back to their pain and suffering? No one seemed to ever really escape from the vicious cycle. It was so depressing.

In fact, right now she was sorry she'd volunteered

her time and it wasn't just because of the throbbing headache. No, the day, the week, had brought back some defeating memories. Nothing ever seemed to change in the family dynamics. All these years of strides against abuse and neglect, and the family members were the ones still in denial. Was it even possible to make positive, lasting changes?

It was damn depressing and it made her question what she was doing spending nights at Tyler's, as if they had something. No one really had something. No one really knew anyone else and she was kidding herself to think so.

Tyler wouldn't stoop to the low-life crimes this man had committed, but he would likely get tired of being married and commit adultery with one of the women who hung around him all of the time. Worse yet, he might get tired of being married and just go through the motions. That would be the most humiliating of all.

Gathering her briefs at the end of a long Friday, Tina decided the plans she and Tyler had made for the weekend were not such a good idea. They'd been spending too much time together. She'd even spent a weekday or two hanging out at his place. Now, she figured she should cut her losses before either of them got in too deep.

I'm just here to get my stuff, she thought, looking in the mirror on the underside of the car visor. "I'm absolutely not staying with him tonight," she told herself, pulling the car into Tyler's driveway, beside his truck, and coming to an abrupt halt.

Taking a deep breath, she unclenched her hands from the steering wheel and went over her game plan. She wouldn't let him sidetrack her with lots of questions. And she definitely wasn't going to let him touch her or kiss her. *Just get the hell outta there.* As she turned the key the engine stopped, but her anxiety built.

After grabbing a shopping bag from the backseat, she slung it over her shoulder. There shouldn't be much to pack. In fact, it was weird for her to leave anything behind.

For a while she'd forgotten where she came from. Big mistake.

She climbed out of the car reluctantly. The garage door was shut so the front door was the only option. With any luck he'd be in the shower or walking the dogs, and she'd just slip in and out, without having to talk to him.

The front door swung open smoothly after she used her key to unlock it, and she hit the security code with sure fingers hoping the buzzing wasn't alerting him to her presence. It was her own fault. She had to go and accept the stupid key and code. What was she thinking! "You have rules and you've gone and broken every one of them," she muttered.

"Who are you talking to?"

"Whom," she told him, even though she didn't have a clue to the proper form of the word when you were caught trying to sneak into a house.

"Okay," he said obligingly. "To whom are you talking?"

"Myself."

He nodded as if he understood. "Rough day?"

"The worst, and I don't want to talk about it. I just came for some stuff. I need to be alone tonight."

Good. Just sound matter-of-fact and be too busy to see him. Maybe she'd take a little trip, and then he'd get used to her not being around. Eventually, his ego wouldn't allow him to say a word. It would be done and relatively painless. It wouldn't even really be a breakup. After all, you couldn't break up what was never formal anyway. It'd just been physical.

She knew she would miss the physical part for a while. Tyler sure seemed to know how to get the job done.

"I'm sorry you had a bad day." He looked at her carefully. "I was just going to take the dogs for a walk. Why don't we grab something for dinner and then head for the beach? We can walk and talk about your day while we both unwind."

It sounded wonderful.

"No thanks. I've got tons of work to do. I don't think I'll be able to take any time off until next weekend or after, so don't worry if I'm not in touch." She walked past him toward the bedroom because her overnight bag with all her favorite makeup and her prescription headache medication, which she really needed right now, was in the bathroom.

"What case did you have today?" Tyler and Ray followed behind her.

Ignoring them both, she paused in the bedroom, looking for her clothing in the closet. The puppy suddenly appeared and jumped up on her to get her attention. She knelt down to run her fingers over his soft coat and scratch his ears. It felt wonderfully soothing.

"He'll miss you while you're gone."

"He'll be fine. You spoil him." She grabbed a pair of her shoes from the closet and stuck them in the shopping bag. She noticed one of her suits hanging in front of his shirt, the one he'd worn to the lobster dinner. They looked so cozy.

Her throat tightened with unwanted emotion. Why in the world had she allowed this to happen? She knew better.

Damn it! She of all people knew about being disciplined. You could achieve almost anything in the world you wanted, but not everything. And not love. Because love was just a fantasy made up to make life more bearable.

"I think there are a couple of thongs in the top drawer." His tone was carefully neutral.

She snatched the suit out of the closet, feeling as if her grip on the plastic was as uncertain as her grip on this reality. How could she be so good at work, and suck so badly at endings? "Thanks, but I'll just get my makeup bag and get going."

"I don't think those thongs will fit me. But I'm kinda fond of the memories." His voice dropped to a murmur. "I can hold them and then rub my hands along the silken edges like I'm stroking your sweet flesh."

The heat was immediate. Pushing him down on the bed and then taking him to the edge would have taken the edge off her day, so to speak. But it would only draw out the drama, and she had to get out. "I don't need the thongs."

I don't want the memories.

"Right now I'm imagining the thong you've got under that prim suit. Since the suit is so conservative, I'm thinking you've got a scalding scarlet thong under there. I want to kneel at your feet, and then while I'm down there I want to pleasure you until your knees are weak, and you can't stand up anymore. I want to carry you to the bed and own your whole body for the night. Then the next time you go into court you'll have a memory to buffer all the stress."

"I doubt it would help the situation." She leaned against the wall by the closet door because her knees were just a little weak.

Frosty made soft sounds of satisfaction as he chewed happily on one of Tyler's shoes. Here was a man who could keep up with her sexually and mentally. He was wonderful and fun. There was tenderness in him, even for dumb dogs. It wasn't irrational that she'd almost fallen for him. Just unfortunate she'd miss him. And the wild sexual ride he'd given her.

Tyler ignored the pup and purposefully invaded her space. "I promise to make you feel so good," he coaxed.

"Back off."

Leaning closer, he told her, "Then just tell me the truth. Why are you running away from me?"

"It's time. We've gotten pretty cozy, and I don't want anyone to get the wrong idea."

"Who is anybody, and what is the wrong idea?"

"Look, I don't want to be interrogated. I've spent all day getting the depositions of the women from the shelter, and I just want to go home and put my feet up on the coffee table. I just want peace."

"And you want to be safe."

"Yes!" She pushed him away and then hurried into the bathroom looking for sanctuary, knowing she wouldn't find any. "Is it too much to ask? This isn't a good idea, and we both know it."

He trapped her against the counter. Only his grasp wasn't sexual. It was tender. He touched her very lightly around the waist and then he brought his hands up to rub her arms gently. His earnest gaze met her eyes in the mirror. "I don't want you to feel safe anywhere else but in my arms."

She ducked her head, making him drop his hands.

He waited until she looked up again before he touched his black eye. "You should feel incredibly safe with this kind of a champion to look after you. After all, I did save the day at the shelter." His tone was playful and mild, but he looked serious when he finished, "I want you to feel safe with me."

"All the women kept saying how heroic you were. You should be flattered." Tina tossed her powder into her makeup bag. Her stuff was scattered across the counter while his was pushed up neatly to the mirror. "Look at this." She gestured. "I'm a slob and you're neat. It's never going to work."

"Opposites attract. Everyone knows that."

"I'll drive you crazy."

"I promise to return the favor." His eyes were deep and earnest. "Each and every night."

She grabbed everything and then stuffed the makeup bag into the bag on her shoulder. Then she turned. He moved back, and she headed toward the kitchen, where she'd left her lucky coffee cup.

Looking impatiently through the cupboards and then in the dishwasher, she turned to him. "What did you do with my cup?"

"Not telling. You'll have to come back for dinner. I picked up salmon and asparagus. I'll give you the cup full of fresh-brewed coffee and ply you with dessert. There are a few other things I've stashed away for future evenings. I thought I might have to negotiate."

Tina felt very confused. No one had ever done so much just to win her over. She pushed her hair back from her face. "Why in the world would you bother?"

"Because I want you."

Okay, that she could understand and handle. She made eye contact and then started unbuttoning her suit coat. "Okay. Let's go into the bedroom and get this over with. I told you that I have a lot of work to do tonight."

He looked very interested as she got down to a lacy scarlet camisole. "Does the thong match?"

"Of course."

He shook his head. "It's still not good enough."

"You want to have sex. I can see it in your eyes." She drifted closer, coat unbuttoned, the thin camisole not hiding the tightening of her nipples. "I want to have sex. Let's get down to the basic ingredients."

She rubbed the front of his shorts; he was fully, beautifully erect. "You don't want this to go to waste."

"I'll make love to you if you promise to stay tonight. You know I'm afraid of the dark." His hand drifted up her thigh. "Have you got on garters?"

"No, thigh-high nylons with elastic."

He slid his fingers up inside the skirt, and she nearly collapsed when he stroked the silk of her flesh and the thong.

"Let's just go into the bedroom. I'm ready."

"I'm enjoying this. In fact, I might just put you up on the counter and make a feast of you." He stroked harder.

"Just hurry."

"Why? So you can run away?"

"Who says I'm running away?" It came out weak and breathless since she was panting with pleasure under the magic of his touch.

"Because I know the signs. Something spooked you today. Just like it has every time I've gotten too close, beyond your comfort zone, beyond all the lines you've drawn to protect yourself. Like the time you let me spend the night." He nibbled her neck and deepened his touch.

"I can't think. I don't want to think," she complained. "Just make me forget."

He pushed her up against the counter so she had to grab the edge with both hands to stay on her feet. Then he pushed the skirt up until it bunched around her waist. Kneeling, he slipped his fingers inside of her, around the thong.

She gasped. "Oh, please."

His touch was deft. He knew her every secret, and his fingers filled her with delicious pressure while he manipulated the thong to slide against her clit.

Intimate kisses as carnal as his touch feathered her thighs. "You are so sweet," he whispered. And then he rested his tongue against the moist material of the thong.

She felt like dessert. She felt everything. Every little nibble until he took her over the edge.

It took her a few minutes to clear her head and straighten her clothing, although he'd pushed her skirt down for her and was leaning against the counter, watching her with a great deal of satisfaction on his handsome face.

"Come here," she said feeling bereft that he'd stepped away from him. "I'm going to return the favor."

"That's not necessary."

"What?" She was confused. He was so aroused his pants were tented and his face was flushed, so what was wrong? "I want to have my hands and mouth on you. I'll do whatever pleases you. I just want to make you feel as good as you always make me feel."

"And then you're planning on running away."

"I just need some space."

"You're afraid."

"I'm not afraid of anything."

"On some level, you do understand why the sex is so urgent with us, don't you?"

"It's not urgent." But she felt as if she'd go up in flames. She wanted him again. All of him. "We're just mature adults who are good at sex. So let's go and experiment so we can get even better."

"It's more than sex."

"No. It's absolutely about sex." She tried to reach for him. "I'll show you."

"Not for me. For me, it's about love."

Tina went totally still as if she'd been caught in a trap. She immediately buttoned herself into the armor of her suit coat. She looked around for the shoes she'd discarded and then bent down to slip them on. "I'm sorry you feel that way."

"Actually, I've found it to be a very heady experience."

"I can't imagine you're delusional enough to believe that nonsense." She crossed her arms over her heart.

He folded his arms, mirroring her. "It doesn't really matter if you believe in it or not. It's a matter of feelings. I didn't plan on falling in love with an attorney," he told her patiently. "I thought I'd look for a woman with more flexibility in her work schedule so that we could have a family. Then I realized you don't really want a family."

"I never said that!"

"I couldn't stop loving you just because you didn't believe in having a family."

"Having at least one child is in my long-term plan."

"You mean that sperm bank nonsense?"

Stung, Tina snapped. "Do you ever wonder if men

will become obsolete when they perfect the dildo? I mean, come on, what would we keep you guys around for? So you can get fat, lazy, and consume beer? I've seen the inside of the so-called American family. My sperm bank idea is actually a calculated solution to the dysfunctional family, which is really the norm."

The cocky bastard laughed. He actually laughed at her.

"Honey, if there were no men on earth, you women would kill each other. Women are competitive, protective to the point of violence, and much closer to their emotions. Men are actually the civilizing factor for women. Women behave themselves to impress men."

"You have a great opinion of yourself."

"No, I have a great respect for women. They are both emotionally and physically powerful—though they play it down so that men aren't intimidated. But you don't. You let it all hang out. I love being challenged by you." He sounded like he meant it.

Tina felt all of her emotions overflow and she wanted—no, needed—to express the fear and frustration that had been bottled up for so long. Listening to the women from the shelter had been like watching her childhood from a front-row seat.

With deliberation she picked up a discarded coffee cup and then smashed it viciously on the top of the marble counter so the pieces flew. "You find me challenging? You want me? Even though you know where I come from?" She looked him dead in the eye. "Don't you think you might want to reconsider the wisdom of those feelings?"

"If we were in court, I would have just made my case," he said smugly. "You're losing control. It's a good sign."

"You think you can manipulate me?" she yelled. "Of course you do. You think I'm dumb enough that making fun of my sex and my ideas will make me *love* you."

"You definitely don't understand love. Because I can't make you love me," he told her earnestly.

"No, you can't. Not ever." Her hands were shaking and she clenched them. Probably just a result of the violence. But he'd brought it on himself. She didn't like feeling threatened, and she'd felt that way since he'd told her that he loved her. Hell, she'd felt that way listening to the women gush and knowing she felt the same sort of hero worship and maybe more.

"Love has to come from inside of you. It's either there or it isn't."

"It isn't."

He went on as if she hadn't spoken. "I think you love me, but you're afraid. Afraid of falling into a pattern you've fought your whole life to escape. But you won the fight a long time ago and now you're free to move on."

"You're damn right I fought to escape, and I've done a good job." She waved her hands for emphasis.

"An amazing job. I have nothing but admiration for your accomplishments."

"I did it on my own. Nobody helped me."

"I know. I'm sorry it had to be that way. I ache for the little girl left all alone in the world."

"I wasn't entirely alone," she admitted in a small voice.

"What?"

"I had an aunt and two cousins."

"Why didn't you go and live with them?"

Tina gathered her courage to admit something to him, something she'd never repeated to anyone. "My cousin once told me the reason my aunt didn't take me in was because my dad's family was white trash."

"She didn't take you because she didn't like your dad?"

She turned to face him. "You don't understand. White trash. My parents might have been just like the people I grew up with. Apparently I *come* from that. I deserve it and I can't take the chance of slipping back into it."

Tyler took her arm and shook her gently. "Tina, stop. That's the craziest thing I've ever heard, even if it's not just an excuse for unbelievable neglect." He grabbed one of her hands and brought it to his face. "People are not born trash. It's what they make of themselves and their lives. I'm sure your parents were good people because look how you turned out without anyone's support."

"What if they weren't good people? What if the only thing keeping me from slipping into that life is my tenacity? What if I relax and let go?"

"You mean if you allow yourself to love me?"

"I can't love you. I can't handle it."

"What if it's the same excuse your aunt used? What if she just couldn't handle having another child? Look what she missed out on because of her fear. Don't you wonder what you'll miss out on if you leave me now?"

She pulled away. "You want to chain me."

"I only want to be with you. You haven't found it confining. In fact, you've found it most pleasurable."

"That's the part I can get from any man."

His face hardened. "Okay. Then why did you come back?"

"For my makeup bag. It has my stuff, my medication." She knew it was a lame excuse. "Okay, even if I wanted to see you it doesn't prove anything. No matter what, I'm doing us both a favor by leaving now before either one of us gets our expectations too high."

"Stay and we'll talk about those expectations. In bed. Entwined and sated."

She shook her head. Her heart was beating very fast. "You can't seduce me."

"I'm done with the seduction. I can only be honest about my intentions. I can only be patient and wait for you to realize you feel the same way. That's the extent of the plan."

She felt her heart sink. Did that mean he didn't want her? "What is this game?"

"I'm going to wait for you to come home." He bent to pick up the puppy and buried his face in Frosty's fur. Then he looked up. "I'm counting on the fact that this mausoleum actually felt like home for a few nights, and on the fact that you really do love me. So I'm going to wait for you."

"Why?" She put two fingernails in her mouth. This was a nightmare.

"Because since I fell in love with you on the cruise, I haven't had any choice. No one else works for me."

She'd felt depressed since the cruise. It had to be the water or something. "You'll get it out of your system."

"If you never come back, I guess I'll have to move on, but I'll wait a while hoping you'll find the courage to come back to me. I just pray you'll use your strength *for* us and not *against* us."

She pulled her fingers out of her mouth. "I have to go," she said desperately. "I can't listen to more of this tonight. I'm sorry. You'll have to make your life work without me."

11

TINA SAT DEJECTEDLY on the back stairs of the shelter. It had never been a refuge before, but she honestly didn't know where else to go. Her place no longer felt like home. It had been a long time since she'd felt so alone and so afraid.

Emma wouldn't approve. She'd tell Tina to go back to Tyler and tell him that she loved him. But Emma didn't understand, not really.

Here, Tina knew she was surrounded by women who were more practical. These women had seen too much to ever urge her to go back to Tyler.

"Honey, you got to get your white ass back to the man you're moping about—if you know what's good for you."

"Go away, Arlene. I don't like talking to you. All we do is fight." *Maybe because we're more alike than I'd like to admit.*

"Because you're so sure you're better than the rest of us."

"If you say so. But at least I can't be bought with new carpet."

"And furniture. Girl, he's the good kind."

"There isn't any good kind. Oh, he's the kind that doesn't hit or humiliate, but he's still a man and men get tired of being tied down. Then they find someone else. Or they blame the woman in their life for everything that's going wrong. Or, my personal favorite, the woman is doing better than the man financially so he starts to bring her down emotionally because he can't compete." Tina rubbed her fingers together and swung her foot in agitation. "Whichever version of the story it's going to be, I don't want a leading role. He's cute, he's ripped and the pup is definitely a draw, but I'm not going for it."

"You loved braiding my little girl's hair. Whatta ya gonna do when you get a hankerin' to have a fancy little girl of your own? You know what it feels like to hold a baby in your arms and know that you don't have to repeat your mama's mistakes?" Arlene's face was flushed. "Even if you end up making worse ones, it's still the best thing you'll ever do."

"There are places you can go. Sperm banks. I'll depend on science to get me a child, and then I won't have to worry about visitation and child support."

"Sperm banks?" Arlene snorted. "Ain't you cold-blooded?"

It stung, no doubt. Arlene had gone to the heart of the matter, and it stung.

"Whatcha gonna do? Look at pictures? Close your eyes and point? How you gonna even hope it's a man with some good in him if you never knew anythin' but his height and his IQ?"

"You get more information than that." Tina didn't know why she was bothering.

"You might be a fancy lawyer, but you don't know nothin' about a person if you don't see it firsthand. At least the man I had, he had some nice days. He might be a mean drunk, but he had some nice days. My little girl, she's got some nice stuff in her, too."

"Would you be spinning your wheels here if you'd gone to a sperm bank?" Tina asked with exaggerated sweetness. Let Arlene think she had all of the answers.

Arlene snorted, gave Tina the finger and then pushed past Tina to get in the back door. The ripped screen door swung shut with a screech.

"I think they need a new screen door."

"Go away, Tyler," Tina said wearily. "Just take yourself away from here. You can't save us."

"That loose part of the screen is probably sharp and it might cut one of the kids, not to mention the nightmares that screeching sound probably causes."

"Why do you want to fix everything?"

"Because I usually can."

She put her hand wearily over her face. "You can't fix where I come from and who I am at the most elemental level. So why pretty it up with new carpets and a screen?" She looked down at her feet, which she'd slipped into an ancient pair of flip-flops. Her pedicure certainly didn't go with the ugly things. "Did Sam call you?"

"No, I called her. I'm not going to let you slip away like everyone else has. I'm not going to do that, Tina. I want to fight for you."

"This is a safe house. All I have to do is call the police."

"And then explain to law enforcement."

"This isn't the same as your black eye, and it won't get you the same sympathy. Please. Can't you just accept my feelings and back off?" Her heart fluttered. He looked so good standing there with his hair brushed casually back from his handsome face. The deep blue shirt brought out the depth of his eyes and she could see he was wearing his heart in his gaze.

She closed her eyes so she wouldn't have to see his pain. *What about your pain? It's going to be so hard to forget him.*

But there were already enough snapshots of him in her mental scrapbook to trip her up. She couldn't afford to get in any deeper.

"You already love me. You can run away, but it's already happened for you." His voice washed over her.

"That's pretty arrogant."

"Yeah. That's one of the ways we fit so well. Besides the sexual ones."

She remembered her bandit, and how he stole her breath away with his technique. Then there was the man at the beach who seduced her with a puppy. The lobster dinner and a fistful of silver balloons. She opened her eyes to blink away the tears.

"Please, go away. If you really love me you'll do what's best for me. No one really escapes the system. I forgot that for a minute, but I remember it now. Let me go before you hurt me more."

"I'm already doing what's best for you. *I'm* best for

you. I can love and care for you all the years of my life. I'll give you a great life. I promise." He put his hand on his heart.

It only made the mist in front of her eyes thicker. "What happens when you get tired of me? When I get tired of you? Then we fight until everything disintegrates to hatred and contempt. If we stay together it's because we're afraid and if we come apart it's because we're afraid."

"Then let's not be afraid."

"Right. That works. Just wave your magic wand and make it all better."

"I told you, fifty percent of marriages last forever."

Not that again. "But how many of those are just going through the motions?"

"I have no idea, but I'm not going to assume we're going to be average at anything we do. We have great communication, argumentation and negotiation skills. I expect our relationship would mean putting those three skills to good use. The thing I don't think is that we'd ever settle for being afraid."

She wrapped her arms around herself, imagining arguing over breakfast, negotiating over lunch and physically communicating on top of the dinner table with various condiments. It sounded amazing. Too bad no one out of the foster care system ever got a happy ending.

Tyler could tell by the mutinous look on her lovely face that he wouldn't win this fight. For the first time, he didn't have a plan. She would never want him. Her closing argument had been very clear. He turned to go out the back gate he'd come in. They needed a lock on the gate, but he wouldn't be around to take care of it. He couldn't even stay in the city—how would he practice law? Tina's little car would ruin his concentration. Her voice in the halls would haunt him. Even the whispered rumors about her new lover would sound like thunder. Maybe he'd go home.

"Where you goin', handsome?" Sam's voice stopped him.

Tyler looked up to see Sam at the back gate like she wouldn't let him through. "I guess I'll try practicing law in Georgia," he told her in a low, dull voice. "I need a change of scenery."

"Our girl giving you trouble?" Sam asked softly.

"Apparently no one who comes out of the system is entitled to a happy ending and they'd be crazy to try for one."

"Yeah, and no little girl who comes out of the system ever becomes a hotshot lawyer who returns to make good for the ones left behind," Sam said in a loud, mocking voice. "It's impossible. I think I'll make it into a fairy tale, and tell these kids every night how they're supposed to get shit jobs and fail at every relationship they try."

"I never said that!"

They both turned to see Tina on her feet, and Tyler had never seen her so angry. Even her hair seemed to be standing on end with the force of her emotions.

"Sam, how dare you say such a wicked thing? I've never done anything but encourage these kids."

Sam nodded. "You've encouraged them with your

very presence. They believe. Now you're gonna tell them that no one can make it."

"I never said anything of the sort."

Tyler's spirits lifted but only a miniscule amount. Tina might be moved to anger, but in the long run she wouldn't listen. She was truly afraid, and his heart ached for her pain, and his.

"I heard you tell the most amazing, handsome man in the world it can't work."

Tyler's lips curved with a smile at the compliment but it didn't go past his face.

"You think we can build a relationship on his good looks?"

Tyler shook his head at his idiocy. He'd known The Shark would be a hard sell, and it was his own fault for trying to capture such a free spirit. Heart in his throat, he moved around Sam to open and then close the gate on a life with Tina.

Tina watched him go with a sinking feeling in her guts. So she pounced on Sam. "I can't believe you. You know what it's like to try to make a hopeless situation work out."

"You've been building this relationship for a while."

Tina chewed on the edge of a nail and felt a chunk of it give way under her teeth. "What are you talking about?"

"You went at it slow after the cruise, but then it sort of gained momentum. You guys did some stuff, had some laughs, took some hits, literally. You already know you're compatible, so why is it so complicated?"

"Because it is."

"Don't you feel more than lust for the boy? Is there nothing deeper going on?"

"Of course I don't feel anything but lust and respect for the man. That's what I've been trying to tell him." Tina felt so relieved. *It was lust and respect, not love. She wasn't tied up in any emotional knots. It was just her imagination and his great sexual technique. She'd be over him in a few days.*

"Yeah girl, and you didn't want to scratch some eyes out when you saw those women fawning over him with his poor black eye?"

"That was just irritation."

Sam sat down on a beat-up lounge chair. Her expressive eyes were soft with sympathy. "I know how it is to be afraid. Tyler, he sends me this guy, and I'm scared to death, but it won't stop me from trying him out, from looking for some happiness in this tough old world."

"Don't go all mushy on me." Tina crossed her arms over her chest. Her fingers rubbed and her foot tapped. She was a mess.

"I'm not going to go mushy on you. I'm just going to give it to you straight. You got no business turning that man down. You need to go after him and let him sweep you off your feet."

"You are crazy."

"You feel different when he's around? Whole? Safe? Complete, comfortable and knocked off balance?"

"Those feelings are contradictory."

"But you feel them. I can see it in your face." Sam

reached out toward her. "You gotta try. For the rest of us poor misfits."

"What am I? A poster child?"

"No, you're the strongest and best. The one who can't let fear keep her down. You love him. You light up like a candle when he's near. You laugh. You got your little girl back."

Tina's brow furrowed. "I don't have a little girl."

"The inner girl. The one who does more than just kick ass. She plays."

"Oh, *you're* the one who suggested all of the childish stuff," she said knowingly.

"Did you play?" Sam pushed her hair back where it fell over her shoulder like a blanket of midnight. "Did you and that boy play like kids?"

"Yes."

"Was it fun? Did you giggle?"

"Yes."

"You know how to relax with him. You know how to play. You know how to fight and I'm guessing you know how to heat up the sheets. It's as much of a head start as anyone ever gets."

"Who are you now, Oprah?"

"Can you imagine never seeing him again? Never kissing or touching him again?"

Tina felt herself beginning to cave. "No."

Sam smiled. "Go home, get beautiful and then crawl to him and beg. I think he said something about moving to Georgia."

Tina's heart stopped. At that precise moment she

knew what a world without Tyler would be like: empty. "He did not threaten to move to Georgia."

"He did. And he's the kind that's as strong as you. If he makes up his mind, he won't come back, even for a pretty lady lawyer."

Tina stood up. "He can't just leave!" It came out as a wail. The thought of being without Tyler left her feeling hollow. Then the hollow filled up with pain. "He's not the kind to run away from a fight! He's not."

"Maybe he doesn't want his life to be a fight. Maybe he just honestly wants to love you and you've made it clear that you don't want that. Case closed." Sam's smile was sadder because of the scar.

"It's not closed." The hollow feeling and the pain threatened to consume her. This was exactly what she'd feared. That she'd come to need him too much. "He can't go."

"Why shouldn't he go?"

"I don't really want him to go!" A tear threatened. Her throat felt tight. Her stomach rolled. "I just didn't want to hurt like this."

"Like what?"

"Like the world's gone dark. Like I can't breathe!"

"Sun is shinin'. And maybe you're having an asthma attack. It sure can't be love. You don't believe in it, anyway."

Tina sank down on the wretched patch of grass they called a lawn. "Then why do I feel like this?"

"You know."

"I already love him."

"Yeah."

"It snuck up on me. I swear it."

"You think they prepare you for this sort of thing in law school?"

Tina tried to breathe. It seemed she had no choice about it. She'd already given her heart. But she did have a choice when it came to what she did about it. Was she strong enough to go for happiness or would she allow her fears to keep her in the dark? "You really think it could happen for me?"

"It already has. Everything you wanted: a kick-ass career, respect, the ability to help others and make a difference, four-hundred-dollar shoes, lots of takeout. You made it, girl. You made it good. Proved everyone who ever said you were nothin' dead wrong."

"Damn right," Arlene called from the house. "Go get him, girl. Not that I don't hope you fall on your fancy face doing it."

Tina ignored the urge to throttle Arlene. "But I don't know what to do about loving him. What now?"

"That's the only thing that's been missing in your life. We've been your family, because we're safe. But you deserve more, family of your own. And girl, Tyler is definitely the cream of the crop. You'd be stupid not to catch him. Go get him. You're The Shark. Use your teeth and nibble your way until he gives it all up."

Arlene snorted from the back doorway. The hole in the screen had more than one curious face looking out, giggling, laughing and smiling. For the moment, all of the women and children looked whole and brave. They were celebrating the moment.

"It's the one thing we've all learned the hard way, Tina. Take hold of the good things and hold on to them for as long as they last. Because without those things it's not only a tough old world, it's hopeless."

Sam's voice. Sam's wisdom from the same school of hard knocks. All these years, Tina thought she'd hidden herself, but now she wondered if perhaps these women saw her more clearly than she saw herself. If these damaged individuals had the courage to grab on to hope after the terrible things they'd gone through, then what the hell was she letting herself off the hook for?

Tina smiled at them, at all of them. And then, trembling, she reached down to put her arms unabashedly around Sam. She even squeezed. "I'm not sure I deserve to be a poster child or that I can make it work," she whispered.

"Promise me one thing." Sam's dark eyes were full of tears.

"What?"

"Just don't forget us, now that you're leaving all your fears behind. We'll be waiting to hear all the gushy details next time you bring pizza."

Tina gazed at Sam misty eyes. "I won't forget you. You all are part of me."

"Not the best part."

Tina looked again at Sam's scar, which made her so tragically beautiful, and she couldn't imagine the courage it had taken for the woman to refuse plastic surgery and wear that badge of courage and pain. "All my life I've been trying to forget the ugly side of myself, to cover it up with expensive clothing and walk in designer shoes. But there's no side of a person without beauty. It's all mixed up."

"That it is, and you got the beauty, the strength, and now the courage. Put it all together and get that guy."

Despite her underlying fear that Tyler would no longer want her, Tina flashed her shark smile. "They don't call us sharks man-eaters for nothing."

NOT QUITE SURE, but determined, Tina rushed through a shower so she'd be fresh and at her best when she saw Tyler. Her hair was mostly dry when she finally shut off the hair dryer, and heard the doorbell ringing and ringing. There was a frantic edge to it.

Dressed in nothing but a light robe and some Ralph Lauren slippers, she ran to the door. It was probably Emma. No one else would be so insistent. What would she tell her? Could she even hold on to her courage and do what she needed to do? Her whole body felt as if it was vibrating with tension. With anticipation.

She opened the door, and her jaw dropped.

The Bandit stood in her doorway, dressed in leather and fur. A mask adorned his face but those blue eyes were unmistakable. He was every woman's dream man—or at least *her* dream man. She put her hands on her hips. "What are you doing here?" she demanded.

"I'm here for my woman, and I'm not taking no for an answer." He moved inside, chains clinking.

Tina looked into the hallway and saw more than one curious neighbor looking out their doors. It seemed she would be a source of amusement for many people tonight. But it didn't matter. Let them watch her grab on to happiness with both hands.

"Did you bring something to tie me up with?"

"Why?" His voice sounded almost hesitant. As if he wasn't quite sure of his reception. "Will I need to tie you up in order to keep you?" He looked her dead in the eye. "I'm almost desperate enough to do it."

"What if I'm not afraid of you anymore? What if you won't need to tie me up to keep me? What if I somehow found the courage to try and make a life with you?"

He pulled the mask off and threw it on the floor. "I wouldn't need a plan? I could just be honest about my intentions?"

"I don't know. I kinda liked your plans."

"What if I plan to tie you to the headboard of your bed and have my wicked way with you?"

"That's a really, really good plan."

Tyler's beautiful eyes lit up. "Tina, I won't settle. First, I'll make you beg, and then I'll make you promise to move in with me. At the first opportunity, I'll get you pregnant so you have to marry me in order to preserve your reputation."

"You promise?"

He picked her up in his arms.

She kicked off her slippers. In his arms she didn't need to pretend she was someone. She didn't need to prove anything. She finally had a home. He was her home, and someone who believed in her, and she would never fear slipping back because she'd be too busy going forward. Forever.

Tyler carried her effortlessly towards her bedroom. "I've captured you. You'll never get away," he told her in his deep bandit voice.

As he laid her on the bed she replied, "Well, then, start putting that claim to good use. I love you so much, I never want to get free."

* * * * *

Happily ever after is just the beginning...

Turn the page for a sneak preview of
DANCING ON SUNDAY AFTERNOONS
by
Linda Cardillo

*Harlequin Everlasting—Every great love
has a story to tell. ™*
*A brand-new line from Harlequin Books
launching this February!*

Prologue

Giulia D'Orazio
1983

I had two husbands—Paolo and Salvatore.

Salvatore and I were married for thirty-two years. I still live in the house he bought for us; I still sleep in our bed. All around me are the signs of our life together. My bedroom window looks out over the garden he planted. In the middle of the city, he coaxed tomatoes, peppers, zucchini—even grapes for his wine—out of the ground. On weekends, he used to drive up to his cousin's farm in Waterbury and bring back manure. In the winter, he wrapped the peach tree and the fig tree with rags and black rubber hoses against the cold, his massive, coarse

hands gentling those trees as if they were his fragile-
skinned babies. My neighbor, Dominic Grazza, does
that for me now. My boys have no time for the garden.

In the front of the house, Salvatore planted roses.
The roses I take care of myself. They are giant, cream-
colored, fragrant. In the afternoons, I like to sit out on
the porch with my coffee, protected from the eyes of
the neighborhood by that curtain of flowers.

Salvatore died in this house thirty-five years ago. In
the last months, he lay on the sofa in the parlor so he
could be in the middle of everything. Except for the
two oldest boys, all the children were still at home and
we ate together every evening. Salvatore could see the
dining room table from the sofa, and he could hear everything that was said. "I'm not dead, yet," he told me.
"I want to know what's going on."

When my first grandchild, Cara, was born, we
brought her to him, and he held her on his chest, stroking
her tiny head. Sometimes they fell asleep together.

Over on the radiator cover in the corner of the parlor
is the portrait Salvatore and I had taken on our twenty-
fifth anniversary. This brooch I'm wearing today, with
the diamonds—I'm wearing it in the photograph also—
Salvatore gave it to me that day. Upstairs on my dresser
is a jewelry box filled with necklaces and bracelets and
earrings. All from Salvatore.

I am surrounded by the things Salvatore gave me,
or did for me. But, God forgive me, as I lie alone now
in my bed, it is Paolo I remember.

Paolo left me nothing. Nothing, that is, that my

family, especially my sisters, thought had any value. No house. No diamonds. Not even a photograph.

But after he was gone, and I could catch my breath from the pain, I knew that I still had something. In the middle of the night, I sat alone and held them in my hands, reading the words over and over until I heard his voice in my head. I had Paolo's letters.

* * * * *

Be sure to look for
DANCING ON SUNDAY AFTERNOONS
available January 30, 2007.
And look, too, for our other
Everlasting title available,
FALL FROM GRACE by Kristi Gold.

FALL FROM GRACE is a deeply emotional story
of what a long-term love really means.
As Jack and Anne Morgan discover,
marriage vows can be broken—
but they can be mended, too.
And the memories of their marriage
have an unexpected power to bring back
a love that never really left....

The real action happens behind the scenes!

Introducing

SECRET LIVES
OF DAYTIME DIVAS,

a new miniseries from author
SARAH MAYBERRY

TAKE ON ME

Dylan Anderson was the cause of Sadie Post's
biggest humiliation. Now that he's back, she's going
to get a little revenge. But no one ever told her that
revenge could be this sweet...and oh, so satisfying.

Available March 2007

**Don't miss the other books in the
SECRET LIVES OF DAYTIME DIVAS miniseries!**

Look for *All Over You* in April 2007
and *Hot for Him* in May 2007.

www.eHarlequin.com   HB314

This February...

Catch NASCAR Superstar **Carl Edwards** *in*

SPEED DATING!

Kendall assesses risk for a living—
so she's the last person you'd
expect to see on the arm of a
race-car driver who thrives on the
unpredictable. But when a bizarre
turn of events—and NASCAR
hotshot Dylan Hargreave—inspire
her to trade in her ever-so-structured
existence for "life in the fast lane"
she starts to feel she might be
on to something!

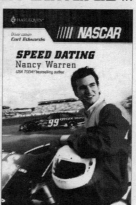

Collect all 4 debut novels in the Harlequin NASCAR series.

SPEED DATING
by *USA TODAY* bestselling author
Nancy Warren

THUNDERSTRUCK
by Roxanne St. Claire

HEARTS UNDER CAUTION
by Gina Wilkins

DANGER ZONE
by Debra Webb

On sale February 2007

---

www.eHarlequin.com   NASCARFEB

HARLEQUIN® *Romance*®

What a month!

In February watch for

Rancher and Protector
Part of the Western Weddings miniseries
BY JUDY CHRISTENBERRY

The Boss's Pregnancy Proposal
BY RAYE MORGAN

Also in February, expect
MORE of what you love
as the Harlequin Romance line
increases to six titles per month.

Silhouette® Desire

Don't miss the first book
in **THE ROYALS** trilogy:

THE FORBIDDEN PRINCESS
(SD #1780)

by national bestselling author

DAY LECLAIRE

Moments before her loveless royal wedding,
Princess Alyssa was kidnapped by a mysterious man
who'd do anything to stop the ceremony. Even if that
meant marrying the forbidden princess himself!

On sale February 2007 from Silhouette Desire!

THE ROYALS
Stories of scandals and secrets
amidst the most powerful palaces.

Make sure to read the other titles in the series:
THE PRINCE'S MISTRESS
On sale March 2007
THE ROYAL WEDDING NIGHT
On sale April 2007

*Available wherever books are sold, including most
bookstores, supermarkets, discount stores and drugstores.*

Visit Silhouette Books at www.eHarlequin.com SDTFP0207

REQUEST YOUR FREE BOOKS!

2 FREE NOVELS PLUS 2 FREE GIFTS!

HARLEQUIN®

Blaze®

Red-hot reads!

YES! Please send me 2 FREE Harlequin® Blaze® novels and my 2 FREE gifts. After receiving them, if I don't wish to receive any more books, I can return the shipping statement marked "cancel." If I don't cancel, I will receive 6 brand-new novels every month and be billed just $3.99 per book in the U.S., or $4.47 per book in Canada, plus 25¢ shipping and handling per book and applicable taxes, if any*. That's a savings of at least 15% off the cover price! I understand that accepting the 2 free books and gifts places me under no obligation to buy anything. I can always return a shipment and cancel at any time. Even if I never buy another book from Harlequin, the two free books and gifts are mine to keep forever.

151 HDN EF3W 351 HDN EF3X

Name	(PLEASE PRINT)	
Address		Apt.
City	State/Prov.	Zip/Postal Code
Signature (if under 18, a parent or guardian must sign)		

Mail to the **Harlequin Reader Service®**:
IN U.S.A.: P.O. Box 1867, Buffalo, NY 14240-1867
IN CANADA: P.O. Box 609, Fort Erie, Ontario L2A 5X3

Not valid to current Harlequin Blaze subscribers.

Want to try two free books from another line?
Call 1-800-873-8635 or visit www.morefreebooks.com.

* Terms and prices subject to change without notice. NY residents add applicable sales tax. Canadian residents will be charged applicable provincial taxes and GST. This offer is limited to one order per household. All orders subject to approval. Credit or debit balances in a customer's account(s) may be offset by any other outstanding balance owed by or to the customer. Please allow 4 to 6 weeks for delivery.

Your Privacy: Harlequin is committed to protecting your privacy. Our Privacy Policy is available online at www.eHarlequin.com or upon request from the Reader Service. From time to time we make our lists of customers available to reputable firms who may have a product or service of interest to you. If you would prefer we not share your name and address, please check here. ☐

HB07